quartet

AF660330

RABINDRANATH
TAGORE

quartet

Chaturanga

Translated from Bengali with an Introduction by

Nirmal Kanti Bhattacharjee

THORNBIRD
NIYOGI
BOOKS

Published by
NIYOGI BOOKS
Block D, Building No. 77,
Okhla Industrial Area, Phase-I,
New Delhi-110 020, INDIA
Tel: 91-11-26816301, 26818960
Email: niyogibooks@gmail.com
Website: www.niyogibooksindia.com

Text © Nirmal Kanti Bhattacharjee

Editor: Mohua Mitra
Design: Shraboni Roy

ISBN: 978-93-89136-13-5
Publication: 2019

All rights are reserved. No part of this publication may be reproduced or transmitted in any form or by any means, electronic or mechanical, including photocopying, recording or by any information storage and retrieval system without prior written permission and consent of the Publisher.

Printed at: Niyogi Offset Pvt. Ltd., New Delhi, India

Rabindranath Tagore (1861-1941)

Poet, playwright, painter, actor, novelist, short-story-writer, essayist, philosopher, educationist, music composer, internationalist, cultural relativist Rabindranath Tagore was a many-splendoured genius, the like of which one comes across but rarely in history. A man of amazing creative efflorescence, with so many facets to it that people are often confused to decide which one is the most important. He has left behind him a body of work that is awe-inspiring and incredible. He is indeed a miracle of nature, the supreme symbol of Indian Renaissance.

Tagore's role as a son, brother, husband, father; his relations with his family, friends, contemporary writers and poets as well as predecessors; his correspondences with the political leaders of his time within the nation as well as abroad; and above all his interpretations about life, revealing his quest for love, faith and devotion, fraught with his deep-rooted anguish, his unfulfilled dreams and expectations...all these still engage us intensely. Here we deal with a man of extraordinary abilities, yet a man having ordinary expectations, who could thereby understand the joys and sorrows of the common man, keeping aside his own gains and losses. And it is for this reason that Tagore remains dear to all people cutting across boundaries, generations, caste, creed or sect.

Introduction

Chaturanga (Quartet) was first published in book-form in 1916. Before that the four chapters of the novel were serialised in the magazine, *Sabujpatra* in 1915 under the tiltles, 'Jyathamashay', 'Sachis', 'Damini' and 'Sribilas'. The first chapter was written when Tagore was travelling in Allahabad and Delhi in December, 1914. The second chapter was partly written in Santiniketan and partly in Surul. The third and fourth chapters were completed in Surul in 1914-15. On 26 December, 1914, in a letter written to Monilal Gangopadhyay from Santiniketan, he mentions, 'This place is not at all conducive for writing.... There are constant obstacles.' And in a successive letter to the same person, he writes, 'I fled Santiniketan for writing the story and had come to Surul. Hopefully I will be able to complete it by day after tomorrow.'

The first English translation of *Chaturanga* was published in *The Modern Review* in four consecutive issues (Feb-May, 1922), under the title 'A Story in Four Chapters' I, II, III and IV. Unfortunately, the name of this translator is still unknown. During the centenary celebration of Tagore's birth, Sahitya Akademi published a new translation by Ashok

Mitra under the title, *Chaturanga* (1963). Unlike Tagore's other novels, this was never dramatised and presented on the public stage. A radio-play was made by Bani Kumar (Baidyanath Bhattacharya) which was aired a number of times from All India Radio.

The structure of *Chaturanga* was quite unique for the Bengali literary scene hundred years back. It is divided into four chapters captioned after the four major characters of the novel, but the entire narrative is presented through the diary entries of Sribilas, the closest friend of Sachis, the hero of the novella. In fact, Tagore was always fascinated by the Bengali quatrain, the classical four-part musical form. He was deeply attached to this form and experimented with it repeatedly in his early stories, culminating in near perfection in *Chaturanga*. Twenty years later, he returned to it with renewed vigour in *Malancha* (The Bower), *Dui Bon* (Two Sisters) and *Char Adhyay* (Four Chapters).

The main character of *Chaturanga* is undoubtedly Sachis, because it is around him that Uncle Jagmohan's entire work-project unfolds; Sribilas's almost blind love as a friend revolves around him only; the victorious smirk in Leelananda's face emanates from winning him over; the flame of desire in Damini's mind is ignited by him, and again it is because of his influence that Damini achieves the final tranquility and peace.

The story of *Chaturanga* circles around the above four characters. Jyathamoshay (Uncle) is an atheist to the core. He totally disregards all the religious practices of Hinduism and runs a social work group to improve the lot of the Muslims and *chamar*s of his neighbourhood. His nephew Sachis and his friend and classmate Sribilas are his two chief disciples and lieutenants in this social service group, much to the dismay of his younger brother Harimohan, Sachis's father, who is a staunch believer not only in Hindu rituals but also in all its superstitions. When Jagmohan died of plague while trying to render medical services to the plague-afflicted underdogs of his area, Sachis's world turned upside down. He left everything behind and became a seeking wanderer. After a long search, Sribilas discovered Sachis in the company of Leelananda Swami, fully immersed in the ocean of devotion, singing and dancing in ecstasy. He would even massage his Guru's feet and make his tobacco as part of service. To be in the company of his friend, Sribilas joins the group and becomes the best-educated disciple of the Swami. After some time, Damini, the beautiful widow of one of Swamiji's disciples joins the group as a part of her departed husband's will. Damini passionately falls in love with Sachis and uses all her guiles to win him over. Sachis, however, considers her an impediment on his path of sadhana, though he is also drawn towards her in some strange way. Sribilas and Damini strike up a natural friendship, much to the consternation of Sachis. In one of Swamiji's sojourns, they had to take shelter in a cave where Damini approaches Sachis in the darkness of the night. Sachis kicks at her chest imagining her to be a primitive beast out to devour him. Tagore uses subtle psychological interpretations of the two minds to lead the relationship towards a path of evolution from the physical to the mystic. Finally, Damini accepts Sachis as her spiritual Guru and marries Sribilas, discovering in him a new soulmate, though she does not live long to enjoy the marital bliss.

The seed of spiritualistic philosophy that Rabindranath paints in this book can be found in an earlier story, called 'Haimanti'. In this story, the author portrays the characters of Haimanti's father and the father-in-law in two different shades of psychological aberration. An elaboration of the same shades we find in the characters of Jagmohan and Leelananda Swami—one defying everything written in the tenets of religion, and the other accepting everything without any question. One follows the European humanism to the hilt and believes work as worship, while the other attaches great value to the meaningless rituals of Hinduism and explains everything in terms of divine ecstasy. That both the paths lead to the futility and destruction is one of the major ideas fictionalised in *Chaturanga*. The struggle of Sachis is against the falsehood of these two worlds.

The other major concept that Tagore attempts to communicate in this novel can be found in the last chapter, titled 'Sribilas'. In trying to explain the relationship between man and God, Sachis tells Damini, 'Damini, don't you understand? The one who sings moves from joy towards rhythm; the one who listens to the song moves from rhythm towards joy. One comes from liberty to binding, the other moves from binding towards liberty. This is how the two sides unite. He is singing and we are listening.'

It seems that Tagore had been contemplating on this relationship for quite some time. In his *Sadhana* series of lectures delivered in the USA in 1913, he writes, 'Last night, in the silence which pervaded the darkness, I stood alone and heard the voice of the singer of eternal melodies...the millions of living atoms of my body will vibrate in tune with the note of the harp-string that thrills at the touch of the master.' ('The Realisation of Beauty', P.144).

In another lecture of the same series, he further elaborates, 'The singer is translating his song into singing, his joy into forms, and the hearer has to translate back the singing into the original joy, then the communion between the singer and the hearer is complete. The infinite joy is manifesting itself in manifold forms, taking upon itself the bondage of law, and we fulfill our destiny when we go back from forms to joy, from love to the law, when we unite the knot of the finite and hark back to the infinite.' ('Realisation in Love' Pp 105-06).

Perhaps I should add a line about the actual business of translation. While translating the novel, what kept me engaged the most is the author's narrative style. A close reading will tell any discerning reader that Tagore never wanted to make the style 'descriptive'. The language he employed is crisp and full of bones and sinews. Even the death of Damini is narrated in two sentences. There is no attempt at pathos or sentimentality. Obviously, Rabindranath wanted to engage our intellect in understanding the novel more than our heart. This is where I struggled the most as a translator. I had to fashion an idiom in English that suited Tagore's playful, often tongue-in-cheek style best. How much I have succeeded in doing so would be determined by the readers' response to this new translation.

At the end, I must acknowledge my gratitude to Tultul Niyogi of Niyogi Books who had a great desire to publish a fresh English version of *Chaturanga*. It is her pure passion for the book that really egged me on to complete this translation work.

—Nirmal Kanti Bhattacharjee

Uncle

I came from a village and got admission to a college in Calcutta. Sachis was pursuing graduate course in Arts at that time. We were more or less of the same age.

Sachis looked like a shining star—his eyes were blazing, his long, slender fingers were like flames of fire; his complexion was like radiance from a halo. When I first saw Sachis, I as if saw his soul; I fell in love with him instantaneously.

It was quite strange that many of Sachis's classmates seemed to dislike him utterly. In fact, those who are ordinary by nature do not fall out with others of his ilk without reason. But when the aura of inner truth shines through a person submerging all crudities, some people devotedly worship him without any reason, while some others constantly hurl insult on him, also without any reason.

The co-habitants of my mess knew that I adored Sachis. This always used to irritate them. They would not miss an opportunity to malign Sachis in my presence. A grain of sand in the eye hurts more if one rubs the eye. I knew it and hence tried to ignore their comments. But one day they went so far in slandering Sachis that I could not hold my peace any longer.

My predicament was that I hardly knew Sachis. The others were either his class-fellows or his neighbours or his distant relatives. They strongly asserted that what they were saying was the infallible truth; I objected equally strongly saying that I did not believe in any of those vilifying remarks. The quarrel just stopped short of my physical drubbing at their hands.

I wept in my bed that night. Next day when Sachis was reading a book half-reclined on the grass by the Gol Dighi during a leisure period, I went up to him and poured my heart out, oblivious of the fact that he did not even know me. Sachis folded the book and held me with a fixed gaze for a few moments. Those who had not seen his eyes would not understand how that gaze felt.

After a while, Sachis said, 'Those who indulge in falsehood do so because they love falsehood and not the truth. Hence, what's the point in trying to disprove what is obviously a slander.'

I protested, 'But look, a liar must be...'

Sachis cut in, 'They are not liars. There is a man in my locality who suffers from palsy. He can't do any work. I gave him an expensive blanket last winter. This made my servant Sibu furious. He came to me and said, "Babu, these trembling fits are all a pretension. The fellow is a cheat." Those who pooh-pooh the idea that I may have any goodness in me are like Sibu. They believe in what they say. An extra costly blanket fell into my lot, and all the Sibus of the world decided that I did not have any right to it. It is below my dignity to quarrel with them on this issue.'

I did not respond to what Sachis said, but asked him directly—'They say you are an atheist, is it true?'

Sachis replied, 'Yes, I'm an atheist.'

I hung my head. I had argued with my messmates that Sachis could never be an atheist.

I received two major shocks about Sachis at the very beginning. Firstly, from his very appearance I thought that he was a Brahmin. His face was like that of a deity carved in white marble. I heard that his caste-name was Mallik. In our village there was a 'high-caste' Brahmin family with Mallik as their title. But later I learnt that Sachis belonged to the community of goldsmiths. As 'high-caste' Hindus, we generally look down upon the gold trader caste. Secondly, we have always considered an atheist a worse sinner than a murderer or even a beefeater.

Speechless, I sat staring at Sachis's face. Even then I saw that radiance in his face, as if a sacred light was burning inside him.

None would have imagined that I would ever take a meal with a goldsmith's son or that I would even surpass my Guru in atheism. Eventually that also was in my destiny.

Wilkins was the professor of English literature in our college. His great scholarship only matched his contempt for the students. He considered teaching literature to Bengali boys in a native college as low as a day-labourer's work. Hence, even while teaching Milton or Shakespeare in a class, he would tell us the meaning of the word 'cat': a quadruped of the feline species. But even he had a different yardstick for Sachis. He would say, 'Sachis, I will make up for your loss in attending this class. Come home, you can have a different fare.'

Fellow students resented such discrimination. They would say, 'The Sahib likes him because he is fair-complexioned and he shows off his non-believer stance to please the Englishman.' Some of them cheekily went up to Wilkins and sought to borrow a book on Positivism with a lot of bravado. The Sahib simply said, 'You won't comprehend it'. That they were found unworthy of even studying atheism further enhanced their indignation against both atheism and Sachis.

2

I put down on paper all the reasons there were for others to castigate Sachis regarding his opinion and conduct. Some of these took place before I knew him, others after.

Jagmohan was Sachis's uncle. He was an infamous atheist of the time. It would not be enough to say that he did not believe in God. Rather, he believed in anti-God. Just as the captain of a war-ship is more concerned with destroying other ships than in stewarding his own, similarly Jagmohan would try to destroy all arguments of the believers. His strategy of debate with a believer was something like this—

'If there is God, then my intellect is his gift;
That intellect tells me, there is no God;
So, God tells me, there is no God;

'And yet you people tell Him in His face that God exists. As a punishment of this sin, a pantheon of three hundred and thirty million gods and goddesses is pulling you by the ear and making you pay the penalty.'

Jagmohan was married when he was a young boy. He lost his wife in his youth. By that time he had read Malthus; he did not marry again.

His younger brother Harimohan was Sachis's father. He was of such diametrically opposite nature that if I described it people would suspect that I was making it up. But while a tale has to move cautiously to win people's belief, truth has no such liability, and hence truth is not scared of being fantastic. That is why, there is no dearth of such instances in real life where elder brother and younger brother are as different as the morning from the night.

Harimohan was a sickly child. Many amulets and precious stones, rituals and incantations, holy water wrung out of mendicants' matted hair, grains of sand collected from sacred pilgrimages, remains of water with which the feet of awesome deities had been washed, benedictions from priests received on payment of hefty fees—all these were made to create a charmed circle to protect him from everything inauspicious.

As a grown-up man he was no longer sick. But the notion that he was weak and needed care lingered. Nobody expected more from him than just staying alive. He did not disappoint anyone, and remained alive and kicking, but kept everyone on tenterhooks with constant threats of falling sick. As his father died at an early age, special attention was bestowed on him by the women of the house. His food was served before all others, his dishes were different from others, his work was much less than others, his rest was much more than others. And why only the mother and the aunts, he believed that he was a special charge of all the gods and goddesses too. Not only gods and goddesses, he paid obeisance to every member of the society according to his or her station, like the daroga of the police post, rich neighbour, highly placed government officer, newspaper editor, and of course to the cow and the Brahmin.

Jagmohan's apprehension was of the opposite kind. He would give the powerful people wide berth lest anyone even suspected that he wanted a favour. This train of thought was also at the back of his mind when he debunked the gods and goddesses. He was totally averse to folding his palm before any power—worldly or divine.

In due course, which means much before due time, Harimohan was married. After three daughters and three sons, Sachis was born. Everyone was surprised by Sachis's close resemblance with his uncle. Jagmohan also possessed Sachis so closely as if he were his own son.

Harimohan was at first happy at the development for sheer material calculation. For, Uncle took charge of Sachis's education. Jagmohan was highly reputed as a scholar of English. Some called him the Macaulay of Bengal, others considered him as the Johnson of Bengal. He was surrounded by English books like a snail inside its shell. Just as the course of a mountain-spring can be traced by the line of the pebbles, his movements within the house could be gauged from the stack of English books rising from the floor to the roof.

Harimohan had spoilt his elder son Purander by over-indulgence. He could never refuse him anything. His heart would always melt for the boy. He felt as if Purander would not survive if prevented from doing whatever he wanted to do. He could not make much progress in his studies. Harimohan married him early, but the marriage could not hold him back from going astray. When the daughter-in-law objected to his conduct, Harimohan would angrily blame her shrewish nature for his son seeking solace outside.

Observing all this, Jagmohan was determined to protect Sachis from the danger of paternal affection. He would not let him go away from himself even for a while. Soon Sachis attained proficiency in English language and literature. But the progress did not halt there. Mill and Bentham ignited his brain to such an extent that he started shining like a torch of atheism.

Jagmohan behaved with Sachis as if they were of the same age. According to him, showing respect to the seniors was a false value; it only trained the human mind to servility. Once a newly inducted nephew-in-law of the family wrote him a letter, traditionally addressing it 'To your gracious feet'. In reply Jagmohan advised him thus: My dear Naren, calling the feet gracious is nonsense as neither you nor I know what it really means. Secondly, you have submitted something only to my feet, but you should know better that the feet are a part of my whole, and as long as these are attached to me, these should not be seen as separate entities. Thirdly, the feet are neither my ears nor hands, hence to offer something to them is sheer madness. Finally, using plural form of my foot you might have expressed veneration, for you people pay obeisance to certain quadrupeds, but it expresses your ignorance about my anthropological identity which I feel I ought to put in order.

Jagmohan discussed such topics with Sachis that are generally considered taboo. If anyone objected to this, he would say that one could drive away the wasps only by destroying their hives; similarly shyness towards these topics could be removed by demolishing the cause of embarrassment. This is what I am doing for Sachis.

3

Once the education part was over, Harimohan tried to rescue Sachis from the clutches of his uncle. But the hook was by then thoroughly stuck in Sachis's throat. As the pull increased from one side, the knot became tighter on the other side. At this, Harimohan got more angry with his brother than his son; he started spreading colourful canards about his brother for tarnishing his image in the locality.

If it were only a matter of beliefs and opinions, Harimohan would not have minded. If after feasting on chicken they had passed it on as mutton, he was ready to condone it. But the two adversaries had gone so far that they could not have been saved even with recourse to falsehood. The incident that really rankled was this:

One of the main tenets of Jagmohan's atheist code was serving the people. Obviously, for an atheist doing good to others involved only his own loss, because there was no piety, no reward, no blessing from any god or grace from any scripture. If anyone had asked him, 'What is your obligation to the greatest good of the greatest number of people?', he would reply. 'That there is no obligation is my greatest obligation.' He used to tell Sachis, 'Look, son, we are non-believers. To maintain this pride, we should keep ourselves completely pure and stainless. Since we do not believe in anything, we must believe in ourselves all the more.'

In his campaign for 'the greatest good of the largest number of people', Sachis was his chief lieutenant. There were a few large leather warehouses in the area. The uncle-nephew duo started a social service campaign among the Muslim dealers and *chamar* workers of those depots. At this the Hindu holy marks on Harimohan's forehead started burning like fire and created havoc in his brain. He knew that talking shastra and Hindu rites with his elder brother would not cut much ice, so he raised objections on the ground of unlawful wastage of ancestral property. His brother said, 'Let my expenditure first come up to the level of your expenses after the pot-bellied priests and *pandas*, only then will I sort it out with you'.

One day it was seen that a feast was being organised in that wing of the house which Jagmohan occupied. All the cooks and servers preparing this feast were Muslims. An enraged Harimohan called Sachis and asked, 'Is it true that you are inviting all your *chamar* friends in this house for a meal?'

Sachis replied, 'If I had the resources, I would have done so. But I have no money. Uncle has invited them.'

Purandar was seething in anger. He declared, 'I will see how they enter this house.'

When Harimohan raised the issue with Jagmohan, he said, 'You make your offerings to your deity every day. I never object. I am making an offering to my god one day. Please do not obstruct it.'

'Your god?'

'Yes, my god!'

'Have you turned a Brahmo?'

'The Brahmos worship the formless. He cannot be seen. You worship the form. He cannot be heard. We believe in the living god; he can be seen, can be heard, you cannot but believe in him.'

'These *chamars* and Muslims are your gods?'

'Yes, these *chamars* and Muslims are my gods. Today you can see with your own eyes the strange power that they have. If you offer them food, they easily take it in their hands and eat it. None of your gods can do this. I enjoy watching this miracle and hence I've invited my gods home today. Had you not been blind to the real god, you would have enjoyed this scene.'

Purandar confronted his uncle and ranted in a high-pitched tone, declaring that he was going to create a bloody ruckus.

Jagmohan laughed and said, 'Look, you monkey, you will realise how powerful my gods are if you just lay your hands on them. I don't have to do anything.'

Whatever bravado Purandar might have been exhibiting, he was more cowardly than his father. His might was there where his childish insistence worked. He did not dare provoke the Muslim neighbours, but went and shouted at Sachis. Sachis stared at the face of his elder brother with his strange eyes, but did not utter a single word in reply. The feast passed over without any ruckus.

4

Now, Harimohan launched a war against his elder brother in an organised way. Their livelihood was maintained from a property which was endowed for defraying the cost of worshipping the house-deity. The two brothers were just beneficiaries by virtue of being worshippers. Harimohan filed a suit in the District Court claiming that Jagmohan being a non-believer should be declared unfit for being a beneficiary of the trust. There was no dearth of prime witnesses. A host of people from the locality was ready to testify.

But all this was not necessary. Jagmohan himself admitted in the court that he did not believe in idol-worship; that he consumed all kinds of food indiscriminately; that he was not aware from which part of Lord Brahma's anatomy the Muslims were created and hence did not see any reason why he should not share a meal with them.

Predictably the Munsif declared Jagmohan unfit for functioning as a *sebait* (worshipper-beneficiary). The lawyers of Jagmohan counselled that this verdict would not hold good at the High Court. Jagmohan told them, 'I won't go for an appeal. I can't hoodwink a god whom I don't believe in. It is those who are dim-witted enough to believe in god that have the cunning to deceive him also.'

The friends were concerned. They asked, 'How would you manage your livelihood? What will you eat?'

He replied, 'If nothing else, air is there'.

Harimohan did not want to celebrate this victory. He was afraid that some misfortune might befall at the curse of his elder brother. But Purandar could not drive out the *chamar*s from this house the other day. That humiliation was still giving him heart-burn. It had now been proven whose god was more powerful. He organised a merry band-party right from the morning. Sounds of drums and cymbals raised quite a din in the locality. An unwary friend had called upon Jagmohan. He queried, 'What's the occasion?'

Jagmohan responded, 'My god is being immersed today with a lot of fanfare.'

Purandar took personal initiative in feeding all the Brahmins of the neighbourhood for two consecutive days. Everyone concluded that Purandar was the true scion of the family.

The ancestral home of Calcutta was partitioned and a high wall was built between the parts of the two brothers.

Jagmohan respected human beings for their instinctive knowledge of which side the bread was buttered irrespective of their religious faith or lack of it. He was sure that his nephew would now desert the pauper uncle and wilfully enter his father's golden cage at least sniffing the smell of food. But Sachis proved that he had neither the religious nor the material gene. He remained with his uncle.

Of course, Jagmohan had held Sachis so dear to his heart and had been so accustomed to Sachis's company that he did not give this development a second thought.

But Harimohan had the slyness to exploit the ego of his elder brother. He went about telling people that Jagmohan was cleverly manipulating Sachis for managing his own mundane requirements.

With a feigned hurt, he would tell people tearfully, 'Can I see my own elder brother starving? But I will never tolerate the devious trick that he is playing by detaining my son. Let me also see how big a schemer he is!'

When this word reached Jagmohan's ears through friends, he got the shock of his life. He cursed himself for not anticipating such a turn of events. He proudly said, 'Goodbye, Sachis!'

Sachis realised the pain with which Jagmohan bade this goodbye. He also understood that there was no point arguing. He had to sever himself from the uninterrupted companionship of the last eighteen years.

When Sachis packed his belongings and loaded them in a carriage for leaving, Jagmohan closed the doors of his bedroom and lay down on the floor. Dusk descended; his old servant knocked on the door for lighting the lamps. Jagmohan did not respond.

Alas, the tradition of greatest good for the largest number of people! The yardstick of science did not apply to human nature. A person may be just one in a head-count, but he could be countless in the matter of the heart. Could Sachis be measured by one, two or three? He pierced the heart of Jagmohan and took his whole world away.

It did not even strike Jagmohan to ask Sachis why he had hired a carriage for loading his luggage. In fact, Sachis did not cross over to his father's side of the house. Instead, he went and took shelter in a friend's mess. Harimohan shed copious tears wondering how his own son could turn a stranger in this manner.

After the partition of the house, a jubilant Purandar installed a deity in their portion of the house, who was worshipped both morning and evening with the blowing of conches and sounding of bells. He was delighted at the thought of how the clamour might be disturbing his uncle.

Sachis started giving private tuitions and Jagmohan found the job of a head master in an entrance school. Harimohan and Purandar tried their best to save the boys of 'bhadralok' families from the clutches of this atheist teacher.

5

After some time, one day Sachis turned up at the first floor study of Jagmohan's house. None of the two believed in the traditional custom of bowing down and touching the feet of elders. Jagmohan rose and embraced Sachis. Once he settled down on a chair, Jagmohan asked, 'What news?'

There was a special news.

Nanibala had found shelter at her maternal uncle's place along with her widowed mother. As long as her mother was alive, there was not much of a trouble. Recently, Nanibala's mother had passed away. The maternal cousins were all louts. One of their friends lured Nanibala away from her shelter. After a few days he started suspecting Nanibala's fidelity and out of sheer jealousy began insulting and humiliating her. The incident took place at the house adjacent to the one where Sachis regularly went for giving tuitions. He was now determined to rescue this wretched girl. But he had neither a place, nor any resources. Hence, he had come to the uncle. To make matters worse, the girl was pregnant.

Jagmohan was furious. If that man were around, he would have crushed his head right away. He was not the type who would calmly deliberate upon the whole situation. He declared forthright, 'No problem, my library is vacant. She can come and stay here.'

Sachis was taken aback. He said, 'Library! But what will happen to the books?'

Before Jagmohan could find any employment, he had sold some of his books to manage his livelihood. The remaining ones could be easily accommodated in his bedroom.

Jagmohan ordered, 'Go and bring the girl forthwith.'

Sachis said, 'I've brought her with me. She is waiting downstairs.'

Jagmohan climbed down the stairs and saw the girl sitting huddled in a corner like a bundle of clothes.

Jagmohan stormed into the room and called out in his baritone voice, 'Come, my dear! Why are you sitting in the dust?'

The girl covered her face with the border of her sari and started sobbing uncontrollably.

Jagmohan did not shed tears easily; today, even his eyes turned moist. He told Sachis, 'The disgrace that this girl is carrying today is my shame, your shame. Alas! Which rascal has put such a burden of shame on her!' Then without any hesitation he caught the girl by both her hands and pulled her up to her feet, saying, 'My dear, you needn't feel ashamed before me. My schoolmates used to call me Jagai, the crackpot. I am still that mad Jagai.'

The border of the sari covering the girl's head and part of the face slipped off. That revealed an innocent teenager whose face bore no stain of disgrace. Just as a flower does not lose its pristine purity even if dust covers it, similarly this girl radiated innocence from her inner core like a rain-tree flower. Her dark eyes were stricken with fear like those of a hunted deer, her whole body was recoiled in shame and embarrassment, but her naïve pathetic face did not betray any trace of sin.

Jagmohan guided Nanibala to his room upstairs and told her, 'Look at the dirty dishevelled condition of my house! The floor has not seen the touch of a broom for long; all things are topsy-turvy; and as for me, there is no routine for a bath or a meal. Now that you've come, things will improve, grace will return to my house, and this Jagai, the crackpot will also turn into a sane being.'

Nanibala had never experienced the warmth and goodwill in human relationships before, not even while her mother had been alive. For, her mother did not treat her just as a daughter, but as the daughter of a widow; the path of that relationship was strewn with the small thorns of apprehension. But how could Jagmohan, despite being a complete stranger, accept her so unreservedly, going beyond the genteel notions of good and bad?

Jagmohan engaged an old maid-servant to help out Nanibala. She was apprehensive if Jagmohan would allow her to prepare his food. After all, she was a fallen woman. But as things turned out, Jagmohan would eat only out of her hands. He refused to eat unless she cooked and served him sitting nearby.

Jagmohan was aware that another scandal was about to break. Nani too realised it and hence passed her days in fear. It started sooner than later. The maid-servant was under the impression that Nani was Jagmohan's daughter. One day, she hurled abuses at Nani and left the job disdainfully. Nani's face turned pale thinking of Jagmohan. Jagmohan said, 'My dear child, the full moon has risen in my house, so it's time for the spring tide of calumny; but howsoever muddy the waves are, my moonlight will remain untainted.'

An aunt of Jagmohan approached him from Harimohan's portion of the house and chided him, 'Shame on you, Jagai! What depravity! Throw out the sinful girl immediately.'

Jagmohan replied, 'You people are virtuous. You can say that. But I am a sinner. What will happen to me if I throw out the sinful girl?'

A distant grandaunt came and suggested, 'Send the girl to the hospital. Harimohan is ready to bear all the expenditure.'

Jagmohan said, 'But she is my Mother. How can I send my Mother away to the hospital just because there is provision for money? How can Harimohan even suggest it!'

The grandaunt was scandalised at this remark. Resting her cheek on the palm of her hand in awe and disbelief, she asked, 'Whom are you calling Mother?'

Jagmohan replied, 'The one who bears a life in her womb, the one who risks her life to give birth to a child. I don't care for the depraved father of the child. The scoundrel only knows how to create trouble for the mother, but himself goes scot-free.'

Hearing this Harimohan shrunk in distaste. He shuddered at the thought of a slut living in his ancestral home, just across the wall. How could he tolerate all this?

He automatically assumed that Sachis was deeply involved in this sin and his atheist uncle was abetting it. With great agitation Harimohan started spreading this rumour to all and sundry.

Jagmohan did not at all try to douse the flame of this unjust scandal. He said, 'In the scripture of the atheists like us, it has been ordained that one would experience the hell of reprehension for doing a good deed.' The more colourful the rumour became, the greater was his amusement. He would laugh out loud with Sachis recounting the new add-on to the calumny. No bhadralok had ever heard that one could laugh about such disgusting matters with one's nephew.

Purandar had never entered the area of the house that fell in Jagmohan's lot since the partition. Now, he vowed to drive away the fallen woman from the locality.

Jagmohan on his part would secure all entrances to the house before he went to school and whenever he got a little leisure he would rush back for a while to check if all was well.

One afternoon, Purandar climbed the wall of their terrace with the help of a ladder and jumped over to Jagmohan's side of the house. Nanibala was taking a nap after lunch. Her doors were open.

Purandar was enraged seeing Nanibala sleeping peacefully and shouted in rage, 'So it's you! You here!'

Woken up, Nanibala's face contorted in fear finding herself facing Purandar. She stood motionless with no energy either to utter a word or run. An angry and trembling Purandar called out, 'Nani! Nani!'

At that moment. Jagmohan entered the room from behind and screamed at Purandar, 'Get out! Get out of my house at once!

Purandar was bristling like an angry cat. Jagmohan said, 'If you don't leave immediately, I'll call the police.'

Purandar glared at Nani for a moment and then left. Nani fainted.

Jagmohan could now guess the whole story. He confirmed it by questioning Sachis. Sachis knew that it was Purandar who had ruined Nani; but he did not have the nerve to disclose it to Jagmohan lest he raised a hell out of anger. Sachis knew that Nani was not safe from Purandar's aggression anywhere in Calcutta. It was only his uncle's place that Purandar would never dare enter.

Nani remained terribly cowered for a few days and constantly trembled like a bamboo-leaf in the wind. Then she delivered a still-born child.

Ever since Purandar had kicked Nani out of the house at midnight, he had searched for her everywhere, but could not trace her out. Now, seeing her at his uncle's place, he was burning in the fire of jealousy. He reckoned that not only had Sachis snatched her away from him for his own pleasure, but he had also kept her under his nose just to spite Purandar. This insult was too much to bear.

Eventually Harimohan got to know the matter. Purandar was not at all abashed at letting him know. Harimohan had always shown some kind of affectionate indulgence to all Purandar's wicked deeds. He found it very unnatural and unholy that Sachis had snatched the girl away from his elder brother. He resolved that Purandar should avenge this unbearable affront and win back his due. He propped up a fake mother for Nani with a bribe and sent her to Jagmohan to tearfully appeal for giving her daughter back. Jagmohan thundered at her with such a terrible countenance that she ran away never to return.

Day by day Nani turned a shadow of her former self, out of fear and anxiety. The Christmas holidays were on and Jagmohan would never go out of the house leaving her alone. One evening, he was reading out a story of Scott to Nani and making impromptu Bengali translations for her benefit, when Purandar stormed into the room with another young man in tow. As Jagmohan was about to call the police, the young man said, 'I'm Nani's brother, I've come to take her away.'

Before replying to him, Jagmohan literally seized Purandar by the scruff of his neck and pushed him out and down the stairs.

Then he turned to the other young man and said, 'You knave! Aren't you ashamed of yourself? You were nowhere there when Nani needed protection and now you turn up as her brother to complete her destruction?'

The man left the place without delay, but shouted from a safe distance that he would rescue his sister with the help of police.

As a matter of fact, this fellow was really Nani's brother. Purandar had called him in to prove that Sachis was the cause of Nani's fall.

Nani prayed to Mother Earth to open up for her to descend and hide her shame.

Jagmohan called Sachis and proposed, 'Let me take Nani somewhere in the North. There I will find out some job. They have let loose such hell that I am afraid the girl will not survive if she stays here for long.'

Sachis said, 'As long as my elder brother is hell bent to cause harm, trouble will follow you wherever you go.'

'What's the alternative, then?'

'There's an alternative. I'll marry Nani.'

'Marry her?'

'Yes, as per Civil Marriage Act.'

Jagmohan held Sachis closely to his chest. Tears ran down his eyes. He has never shed such tears in his mature age.

6

After the partition of the house, Harimohan had never visited Jagmohan. That day he came to Jagmohan's part, distraught and dishevelled, and asked. 'Dada, what is this impending calamity I hear of?'

Jagmohan replied, 'Calamity was indeed about to happen. Now, ways are being devised to avoid it.'

'Dada, Sachis is like your son. How can you marry him to that slut?'

'I've brought up Sachis like my own son. Today, he has brought me glory. My effort has been crowned with success.'

'Dada, I accept defeat. I'll execute a deed bestowing half of my regular income to you. Please do not take such terrible revenge upon me.'

Jagmohan rose from the chair and said, 'Really? Are you trying to lure a dog by throwing left-overs to it? Mind you, I'm not a pious person like you, I'm an atheist. We don't avenge our insult nor accept any favour.'

Harimohan then went to Sachis's mess and taking him aside, he exploded, 'What the hell are you up to? Must you blot the family name in this way? It's worse than death.'

Sachis replied, 'I'm trying to erase the blot on the family. Otherwise, I've no desire to marry.'

Harimohan tried another route. 'Have you lost all your sense of ethics? That girl is like your elder brother's wife. And you—.'

Sachis cut him short, 'Wife? Please do not even utter such falsehood.'

At this, Harimohan hurled some of the choicest abuses at Sachis. Sachis did not reply.

Harimohan had a serious dilemma. Purandar had shamelessly declared that if Sachis married Nani, he would commit suicide. Purandar's wife retorted, 'That will be a good riddance. But you don't have such guts.' Not that Harimohan was totally convinced by Purandar's threats, but still he lived in fear.

So far Sachis had avoided Nani. He had never met her alone, nor had he spoken to her more than one or two sentences. Now that the marriage proposal was finalised, Jagmohan told Sachis, 'You should have a detailed talk with Nani in seclusion. Both of you must know each other's minds clearly.'

Sachis agreed.

Jagmohan fixed a day. He told Nani, 'My dear, today you'll have to dress according to my wish.'

Nani hung her head bashfully.

'No my dear, this is my one desire. I will like to see you properly decked up today. You've to fulfil this desire.'

He handed over to Nani a gold-worked sari of Benaras with matching blouse and veil, which he himself had purchased for her marriage.

Nani bowed down to his feet. He moved his feet away in embarrassment and said, 'I haven't been able to cure your devotion even after so many days. Well, I agree that I'm older to you in age, but I've looked upon you as a mother. So, you are above me.'

He kissed her forehead affectionately and said, 'I've an invitation to Bhabatosh's place. I may be late to return.'

Nani held his hand and pleaded. 'Father, please give me your blessings today.'

'Ma, I foresee that you will convert this non-believer to a believer. I don't believe in blessings at all, but when I look at your face I feel like blessing you.'

Saying this, he lifted her face with his fingers and looked at her intently for a while. Tears ran down Nani's cheeks.

At dusk, a messenger ran to Bhabatosh's house and fetched Jagmohan back home. He saw Nani's body lying flat on the bed. She was wearing the dress he had given her. There was a letter in her hand. Sachis stood beside her.

He opened the letter and read:

'Father, I couldn't do it. Please forgive me. So long I have tried my best thinking only of you. But I haven't been able to forget him till today. A billion obeisance at your lotus feet.

—Nanibala, the sinner.'

Sachis

The atheist Jagmohan told Sachis before his death, 'If you have any lurking desire to perform the funeral rites, do it at your father's death, not mine.'

The events leading to his passing are as follows.

The year in which Calcutta first saw the epidemic of plague, people were more scared by the liveried minions of the hospital than by the plague itself. Harimohan thought that the plague would first afflict his *chamar* neighbours, and through them his family also would be infected. Before fleeing his home, he approached Jagmohan, 'Dada, I've found a house near the Ganga at Kalna. If you—'

Jagmohan, 'Of course you should go. But how can I leave these people behind?'

'Whom?'

'These *chamars*, of course.'

Harimohan pulled a face and left. He met Sachis at his mess and pleaded, 'Come along with me.'

Sachis said. 'I've work to do here.'

'What work? Cremating the *chamars*' corpses?'

'Yes, if necessary—'

Harimohan flew into a rage and said, 'Yes, indeed! If necessary, you can pave all your ancestors' way to hell! You, scoundrel, idiot, atheist!'

Taking all this as signs of approaching doomsday, he returned home in despair and wrote the name of Goddess Durga in small hands a thousand times to propitiate the powers above.

Harimohan left home. Plague broke out in the locality. People were scared to call a doctor lest they were despatched to the hospital. Jagmohan himself went to inspect the condition of the special hospital set up for plague. Disgusted at what he saw, he said, 'It's not a crime to fall sick.'

He set up a private hospital at his own house. Along with Sachis, a couple of us volunteered to serve as nurses. We had even a doctor among us.

The first patient to enrol in our hospital was a Muslim who died. The second patient was Jagmohan himself; he also did not survive. Before breathing his last, he told Sachis, 'I've extracted the final *bakshish* for the religion that I have believed in so long. I've no regrets.'

Sachis never bowed down at his uncle's feet during his life-time. After his death, he did so for the first and the last time.

Later, when Sachis met with Harimohan, the latter commented. 'The atheists are destined to die in such a fashion.'

Sachis proudly replied, 'Yes, they are.'

2

If a sudden whiff blows out a lamp, its glow is extinguished at once. Jagmohan's death had the same effect on Sachis. We did not even know when and where he disappeared. I lost all trace of him.

It was not easy for us to gauge how dearly Sachis had loved his uncle. He was Sachis's father, friend and even son. For, he was so indifferent to his own welfare and so unaware of the ways of the world that Sachis had to protect him from all possible harm. Thus, whatever Sachis had got from life was through the uncle and whatever he had given was also through the uncle. It would be impossible to imagine what Sachis passed through with the void created by his demise. During that intolerable mental turmoil Sachis was desperately trying to analyse how the void could be so absolute; how could there be such a terrible chasm where no truth lasted? If the negative in one sense is not balanced by the positive in another, the whole world would turn into a big zero.

Sachis restlessly travelled from one place to another for two whole years. I could not find any information about him. However, we continued our mission with greater vigour. We would officiously challenge whoever was doing any work in the name of religion and would start doing such select 'good' works that no bhadralok would ever speak well of us. Sachis was the flower amidst us; as he withdrew himself, all our thorns lay bare and bristling.

3

We did not get any news of Sachis's whereabouts for two years. I would usually never want to speak ill of Sachis, but I could not help thinking that the level at which his mind was tuned had gone down by the jolt of Uncle's death. Once, on seeing a mendicant, Uncle said, 'Just as a pawn-broker clinks a coin to test it, life also sounds out a man by inflicting loss, bereavement and temptation of salvation. Those coins which give out a weak sound are thrown away by the pawn-broker; these hermits are the thrown-away fake coins, worthless in the business of life. And yet, they show off as if they have renounced the world. One who has even a minimum ability has no way of escaping from life. Dry leaves fall from the tree, because the tree sheds them, as they have turned into garbage.'

Had Sachis of all people fallen to the category of garbage? Had it been scripted in the black touchstone of sorrow that Sachis had no more demand in the market called life?

At that time, news came about that Sachis–our own Sachis–was dancing in a trance, cymbals in hands, singing the praise of God with Leelananda Swami in some place near Chittagong. There was a time when I could not figure out how a person like Sachis could be an atheist. Today I could not figure out how Leelananda Swami could make a person like Sachis sing and dance in a religious congregation!

Where do we hide our faces now? The enemies would laugh at us and there was no dearth of enemies. Young men of our group got extremely agitated against Sachis. Many went to the extent of saying that they had always suspected that Sachis had no substance; it was all hollow emotion.

I now came to realise how much I loved Sachis. He had delivered such a deathly blow to our group and yet I did not feel any anger against him in my mind.

4

I set out in search of Leelananda Swami. After crossing many rivers, passing many fields, spending many nights in wayside shops, I found Sachis in a village. It was around two in the afternoon.

I wanted to meet Sachis alone. But that was not possible. The courtyard and veranda of the disciple's house where Swamiji had accepted hospitality were chock-a-block full of devotees. There was kirtan through the whole morning. Arrangements of a meal for the people who had come from afar were in progress.

As soon as he saw me, Sachis rushed to me and embraced me tightly. I was taken by surprise. Sachis had always been restrained. The depth of his feeling was displayed in his calm composure. Today I felt as if Sachis was intoxicated.

Swamiji was taking rest inside the house. The door was ajar. He saw us and called out in a deep voice, 'Sachis!'

Sachis hurried into the room. Swamiji asked, 'Who is he?'

Sachis replied, 'My friend, Sribilas.'

By that time I had earned some fame or notoriety. On listening to one of my English speeches, a scholarly Englishman commented. 'What a—', but let me not multiply the number of my enemies by narrating all these details. That I was a hardcore atheist and that

I could speak English at a speed of twenty to twenty-five miles per hour was well known not only amongst the student community but among their parents too.

I believe Swamiji was quite happy at my arrival. He summoned me. Entering his room I did a formal namaskar, in which, though my palms rose like a falchion and touched my forehead my head did not necessarily bend down. We were followers of Uncle; our namaskar, like a bow without string, had shunned the bowing part and become dangerously vertical.

Swamiji noticed it and told Sachis, 'Get me my hookah, Sachis.'

Sachis sat down to prepare the tobacco for the hookah. As the cinder started burning in the bowl, I was also burning inside. I did not know where to sit. As furniture, there was only a plain wooden cot on which Swamiji's bed had been made. I supposed there was nothing wrong in sitting upon it, but somehow I did not feel like. So I kept standing near the door.

It seemed Swamiji was aware that I was a Premchand-Roychand scholar. He said, 'My child, the diver reaches down to the depths of the ocean to collect the pearl, but it will be disastrous if he gets stuck there. He has to come up to breathe. Similarly, if you want to survive, you also must come up from the depths of the ocean of your book-learning to the world above. You were a Premchand-Roychand scholar once, it is now time to seek your release from it.'

Sachis handed over the pipe of the hookah to him and sat down at his feet. He immediately spread out his feet and Sachis started kneading them lightly.

This sight hurt my emotions so deeply that I could no longer stay back in the room. I realised that asking Sachis to prepare the tobacco, massage the feet were all specially designed to shock me.

As Swamiji rested, the visitors had a filling khichri lunch. The kirtan commenced at five again and continued till ten at night.

At last when I had Sachis alone at night, I told him, 'Sachis, you have been brought up in total liberty; how come you've tied yourself in such bindings today? Was Uncle's death such an absolute death?'

Sachis replied, 'Sri, as long as Uncle was alive he gave me liberty in life like a child who enjoys liberty in its playground. With his death he has given me my liberty in the ocean of divine ecstasy, like a child who enjoys freedom in its mother's lap. I've enjoyed that liberty of my daylight hours; why should I miss out on this liberty of my twilight moments? Please be assured that both these elements are gifts from my uncle himself.'

I grumbled, 'Whatever you may say, Uncle would not have approved such habits like preparing a tobacco bowl or massaging someone's feet. This does not look like liberty to me either.'

Sachis countered, 'But that was a freedom on the solid earth. Uncle trained my hands and feet in the field of work; whereas this is the sea of ecstasy, where the way to freedom is through the boat alone. This is why my Guru holds me fast in his service; I am sailing across the sea by massaging his feet.'

I said, 'It doesn't sound so bad when you say so, but what about the man who stretches his feet purposefully towards you—'

Sachis interrupted me, 'He can do so, because service is not required by him. If he had, he would have felt ashamed to do so. It's my requirement.'

I realised that Sachis was in a different world where I had no entry. The person whom Sachis took in his arms immediately on sight was not Sribilas; he was everyman; he was an idea.

Such ideas work like intoxicants. An inebriated person can embrace anybody and shed tears in his drunken stupor, whether it is you or somebody else. However, in this act of hugging me, whatever pleasure the drunk might get, I did not get any. I had to be just a wave in that flood of oneness. But I had my own identity.

I realised that argument would not lead me anywhere. But it was not possible for me to leave Sachis in that state. For being with him, I also started moving with the congregation of disciples from village to village. Gradually, the intoxication infected me too; I also embraced everyman in my chest, cried in ecstasy during the chanting of the kirtan, massaged the feet of the Guru and one day suddenly, in an emotional state of mind, witnessed Sachis transfixed in a trance, exuding a divine glow.

5

Leelananda Swami's charisma spread far and wide, courtesy his conversion of two formidable English scholars and atheists like us. His disciples in Calcutta now started pestering him to move to the city and settle down.

He came to Calcutta.

He had at one time a devotee called Sibatosh. Swamiji used to stay at his house in Calcutta. The greatest joy in Sibatosh's life was to serve him along with his whole entourage. When he died, he bequeathed that house and all his property to his Guru along with his young, childless widow. It was his wish that eventually this house would become the main centre of the sect and their activity. We all put up in this house.

It was one kind of life-style when we were singing and dancing through the villages. In Calcutta, it was difficult for me to keep up the same tempo. So long I was in a world of ecstasy where a transcendental love-game between the universal feminine and the eternal male mind continued. It is that tune which permeated every manifestation, be it the village pasture, the shade of the banyan tree by the river-bank, the lazy leisurely noontide and the stillness of the evening trembling with the cricket's stretched hum. I was as if dream-walking through the open space, unobstructed. And now suddenly my head was knocked by the hardness of the city, the crowd of humanity pushed me around. I was jolted awake from my reverie.

It was in a mess in this city of Calcutta that I pored day and night over books, endlessly argued about the future of the nation with friends at Gol Dighi, worked as a volunteer in political conferences and almost landed in jail fighting against the injustice of the state. It is here that we had taken a vow at the call of Uncle that we would resist all kinds of exploitation by the society; would emancipate the nation's soul from slavery of thought. It is through the vast populace of Calcutta that I had trodden my path with head held high, daring the wrath of people known and unknown, like a boat boldly sailing upstream. I desperately tried to sustain that tearful emotional state of mind in this crowd of Calcutta with her strange tangle of hunger and thirst, happiness and sorrow, good and evil. I felt low every now and then, thinking that I was weak. I felt guilty thinking that there was no discipline in my religious practice. I looked at Sachis. His face did not betray any consciousness that there was a city called Calcutta somewhere in this world. All this was illusion to him.

6

We two friends started living with our Guru at Sibatosh's house. We were his principal disciples. He did not want to be separated from us.

We discussed divine ecstasy and its philosophy with our Guru and brother disciples day and night. During those deep discourses one would occasionally hear snatches of full-throated laughter of a woman from the inner chamber of the house. Sometimes one would hear someone calling loudly—'Bami'. These are trifles in the high level of consciousness where we had strung our minds, and yet they would seem to me as if there was a sudden shower of rain in the midst of drought. When tell-tale hints of life would touch us like torn petals of flower from the invisible other side of the wall, I would suddenly feel that the true world of ecstasy lay there, where the bunch of keys jingled from the corner of Bami's sari, where the aroma of spices rose from the kitchen, where broom sounded at the floor, where everything was trifle but true, where there was a blending of all the sweet and the bitter, the fine and the coarse, the tender and the pungent.

The widow's name was Damini. I saw her in flashes, fleeting across the doors and curtains. However, we two friends were so much at one with our Guru that after a little while there remained no barrier of segregation between us and Damini.

Damini was like the lightning inside the rain clouds of the month of Sravan. Outwardly she was a well-endowed young woman; inside her burnt a restless fire.

In Sachis's dairy it was written somewhere:

'I have seen one archetype of womanhood in Nanibala—the woman who accepted the stain of impurity on herself, who sacrificed her life for a depraved person, who filled the cup of life by her death. I have seen another archetype of womanhood in Damini; this woman is not attracted to death. She enjoys life to the hilt. She is blossoming more and more with beauty and fragrance like a spring flower. She refuses to give up anything; she is unwilling to accommodate a renunciator in her home; she has vowed not to bow down to the austere freeze of the northern wind.'

Let me narrate here the background of Damini. She was married to Sibatosh at a time when her father Annadaprasad's jute business had flourished phenomenally, yielding ample profit. So long Sibatosh had high birth as the only capital, but now fate smiled at him. Annadaprasad gifted him a house in Calcutta and made provisions so that he could live in comfort with his wife. Moreover, he gave Damini jewellery worth a fortune.

Annadaprasad tried his best to train Sibatosh in his own trade. But Sibatosh was rather indifferent to worldly affairs. An astrologer had told him that at a particular day and time when Jupiter would be favourably placed at his planetary position, he would achieve salvation. From that day onwards he gave up all desire for wealth, wine and woman, and embraced the path of austerity. Eventually, he turned into a disciple of Leelananda Swami.

Meanwhile, Annadaprasad incurred heavy losses in business. The reversal of fortune forced him to sell off everything including his house. The situation became so desperate that starvation stared at his and his family's face.

One evening Sibatosh came to the inner quarter of his house and asked Damini, 'Come with me. Swamiji is here. He wants to talk to you and give you some counsel.'

Damini replied. 'I'm busy. I can't go now.'

Sibatosh came closer and saw that Damini had taken out her jewellery box and was rearranging the items.

'What are you doing?' he asked.

Damini said, 'I'm putting my ornaments in proper order.'

Sibatosh thought, she had no time for Swamiji just because of the ornaments! That's not done.

Next day Damini found her jewellery box missing from the chest.

She asked her husband, 'Where are my ornaments?'

The husband replied, 'You've offered them at your Guru's feet. This is why he called you yesterday. He can read our minds. He has now rid you of your greed for gold.'

Damini became furious and shouted, 'Give me back my ornaments.'

Sibatosh asked, 'What will you do with them?'

Damini said, 'These are my father's gifts. I'll return them to him in his need.'

Sibatosh said, 'They are now in better hands. Instead of aiding a materialist they would serve the cause of the faithful.'

In this way, exploitation by faith started. Damini was required to be totally liberated from the ghosts of all earthly desires. Hence, exorcists were constantly working on her mind. While Damini's father and kid-brother were starving, she had to cook for sixty to seventy devotees every day at her home. She had deliberately not added salt to the curry, she had wilfully allowed the milk to burn—and yet the rigours of her spiritual discipline continued.

The final punishment for her lack of faith was meted out by her husband when at the time of his death, he left his wife along with all his property to the special care of the Guru.

7

There were ceaseless waves of faith in the house. People from far and wide were coming to find solace at the Guru's feet, while Damini got the opportunity of being near to him without any effort. And yet, she trounced and neglected that rare privilege day and night.

When the Guru sent for her for a special session of discourse, she would pretend headache. When he pointed out some serious lapses in the arrangement of the evening session, she would reply that she had gone to the theatre. This reply was not factual but provocative. The women devotees were particularly amazed at Damini's conduct. Neither did she dress like a conventional Hindu widow, nor did she care for the Guru's discourse sessions. Moreover, she did not betray any glow of piety and purity that automatically rubbed off on you if you were in the company of such a great saint. Everyone unanimously agreed that they had never seen such a strange woman.

Swamiji used to take it in his stride. He would say, 'God likes to fight with only those who have strength. There will be no words in her mouth, the day she succumbs.'

He started readily absolving her of all her insolences. Damini was all the more perturbed by that forgiveness, because it was tantamount to another form of admonishment. One day, the Guru even overheard Damini mimicking the special sweet tone in which he used to talk to her. She was having a good laugh with her companions.

Still he said, 'The miracle will happen, and for demonstrating it, God is using Damini just as a medium. The poor girl has no fault of her own.'

When we first reached there, we found Damini in that condition. Then miracle really started happening.

I do not feel like writing any more; it is not easy to write either. The pattern of pain that is woven by an invisible hand from behind the screen of life does not follow any theory or any commissioned design. This is why there is discord within and without; there is so much suffering, there are so many tears.

One could only wonder, by which rays of the dawn Damini's rough shell of revolt was totally shattered and she lifted her dew-washed face upward like a flower of consecration. Her service was now so smooth and graceful that its sweetness came as a boon to the Guru and his devotees.

Thus when Damini was blossoming like a lotus, Sachis began to notice her grace. But what I am trying to say is that Sachis only saw her grace, but did not see Damini.

There was a photograph of Leelananda Swami in meditation, framed in a porcelain panel in Sachis's drawing room. One day he found it lying shattered on the floor. Sachis thought that it was the mischief of his pet cat. But many more such incidents kept happening that even a wild cat could not have caused.

There was a restlessness in the atmosphere around, while an invisible lightning coursed underneath. I do not know about others, but my mind was full of pain and agony. At times I thought of running away from all this, as the waves of this ecstatic pleasure were too much for me. In comparison, my dry discourses on the Bengali alphabet with the *chamar* boys were much better.

One winter afternoon, when the Guru was taking rest and the tired disciples were also relaxing, Sachis went to his bedroom looking for something. It was an untimely visit and he came to an abrupt halt at the threshold of the room. Damini was down on her knees, waves of her long hair spread around. She was knocking her forehead on the floor, saying, 'O stone, o you stone, have mercy on me, have pity, kill me.'

Sachis's whole body trembled in fear. He turned around in a flash and rushed back.

8

Once every year Guruji used to go to a secluded place for a few days for meditation. In the month of Magh, the time for the trip approached. Sachis said, 'I would like to come with you.' I said, 'I would also like to come.' I was tired to the marrow by the fever of ecstasy. The prospect of the strenuous travails of travel and life in solitude appealed to me much.

Swamiji called Damini and said, 'My dear, I will go for a trip. Like previous years, let me arrange your stay for this period with your aunt.'

Damini replied, 'I will come with you.'

Swamiji said, 'It is a difficult journey. You won't be able to stand it.'

Damini said, 'I will manage. You don't have to worry about me.'

Swamiji was pleased with this new-found devotion of Damini. In other years, she used to eagerly wait for these days. This was her holiday time. Swamiji thought, what a miracle! How even a stone came back to life by the divine alchemy!

Damini did not budge. She came along with us.

9

We walked in the sun for almost six hours that day and reached a place which was a cape on the sea. It was totally quiet and solitary; only the soft murmur of the idle waves breaking on a calm sea, mingling with the breeze of the coconut groves. The cape looked as if a tired arm of the sleeping earth had spread across the sea. On the palm of that hand, there was a small bluish-green hill. There was an ancient cave sculpted out of the base of the hill. A heated debate was going on among the scholars whether it was a Buddhist or a Hindu cave, whether the sculptures carved on its walls were of Buddha or Vasudeva and whether there was influence of Greek art on them.

It was earlier decided that we would see the cave and then go back to the nearby village. But that possibility turned remote. It was almost dusk. Moreover, it was the twelfth day of the new-moon. Guruji said, 'We shall spend the night in the cave'.

We three sat down on the sand under the green covering. On the western side of the sea, the setting sun bowed down, as if offering its last salutation to the imminent darkness. Guruji started singing—he could often sing from the writings of modern poets—

On the way I united with you
At the end of the day
The twilight glow vanished in a trice
As I set my eyes on you.

The song deeply moved all of us. Tears rolled down Damini's eyes. Swamiji started the *antara*—

Whether I see you again or not
I would not grieve for that
Stay awhile—
let me cover your feet with my flowing hair.

When Swamiji stopped, the silence of the evening spread across the sky and the sea swelled by the tune of the song like a fully ripe golden fruit. Damini bowed down at the Swamiji's feet for a long time, her long hair spreading across the sand.

10

Sachis's diary records the following:

'There were many cells in the cave. I spread my blanket in one of these and lay down. The darkness of that cave was like a primitive black animal—its wet breath was as if touching my body. I felt as if it was the first primordial animal with no eyes, no ears, but only an atavistic hunger; it was imprisoned in that cave for endless time; it had no mind, no awareness of anything; it only had pain—it cried silently.

'Exhaustion sat heavily on my body like a weight, but sleep eluded me. A bird, most likely a bat, flapped its wings and moved in and out from the dark, into the dark. I had goose pimples over my whole body as the wind from its flapping wings touched my body.

'I thought of going outside and sleeping in the open. But I could not gauge in the darkness which side the opening of the cave was. As I crawled towards one direction and I hit my head on the stone wall; when I crawled in the opposite direction, I fell in a small ditch where the water seeping through the wall had collected.

'Finally I returned to the blanket and lay on it.

'It seemed that the primitive beast had captured me in its mouth within its dripping saliva, there was no way out. It was like a dark hunger; it would lick my body little by little until no flesh remained. Its secretion would gradually consume me.

'Oh God, let me pray for some sleep; my consciousness was unable to cope with the stifling embrace of that disastrous darkness, of which death was the only match.

'I did not remember after how long a thin blanket of numbness spread over my consciousness—it was perhaps not sleep proper, but a trance. At one point, in that stupor I felt a deep breath near my feet. My body turned cold in fear. Must be that beast!

'Then something grabbed my feet. First I thought it was the wild animal. But they usually had fur on their body—this one did not. My whole body shrank. I imagined it to be a strange reptile. How was its head, how the body, the tail, what was its way of devouring—I knew nothing. It was more despicable because of its softness, that cluster of hunger.

'I choked in fear and distaste. I started pushing it with both my feet. I felt it had placed its face on my feet...it was breathing heavily...I did not know what kind of face it had. I kicked out at it repeatedly.

'At last my trance broke. Earlier I had thought there was no fur on the beast's body. But suddenly I felt a heap of mane over my feet. I sat bolt upright.

'Someone slunk away from the cave in the darkness. I thought I heard a sound. Was it a suppressed cry?'

Damini

We returned from the cave. Our accommodation was arranged in the first floor rooms of the house of one of Guruji's disciples near the village temple.

Damini was not to be seen much after our return from the cave. She cooked for us and did other household chores, but would not appear before us as far as possible. She had made friends with the women of the neighbourhood and spent the leisure time visiting one house or the other.

Guruji got a little perturbed. He thought, Damini was more inclined towards the nest, not much towards the sky. For some days, she served us with a lot of devotion, but now she had grown weary of it. There were lapses in her work, that natural grace was missing.

He grew a little apprehensive of her. There was a deep frown in Damini's brows for the last few days and her mood had also become quite unpredictable. At the turn of her neck under the loose knot of hair on her shoulder, in her tightly pressed lips, in the corners of her eyes, in the frequent flings of her hands, one could detect hints of a serious revolt.

Guruji immersed himself again in songs and kirtan. He hoped that the truant bee would again come and settle on the honey-pot, being attracted by the sweet smell. The shorter days of autumn were overflowing with the intoxication of music.

But Damini was still elusive. Noticing this, one day Guruji smiled and said, 'God is a-hunting. The roe is enhancing the pleasure of hunting by constantly fleeing. But she has to give in.'

When we had first known Damini, we hardly noticed her absence during the kirtans and discourses. But now her absence made her more conspicuous. That she was not visible was a reality that hit us like a gust of wind. Guruji had surmised her absence as her vanity and hence, this was hurting his own vanity. As for me—perhaps I need not tell you what I thought.

One day, Guruji summoned his courage and asked in a very mild tone, 'Damini, do you have time this evening? In that case...'

Damini said, 'No.'

'Why, may I know?'

'I have to go and prepare sweets at a neighbour's place'.

'Why sweets?'

'There is a wedding at the house of the Nandis.'

'Is it absolutely necessary for you...'

'Yes, I have committed.'

Without saying anything further, Damini left like a gale storm. Sachis was dumb-founded at this conduct of Damini. A lot of highly placed people, rich and learned, bowed down before his Guru. How could this chit of a girl behave with so much insolence?

On another evening, Damini was at home. On that day, Guruji was speaking on a particularly sublime topic. After a few minutes of discourse, he looked at our faces and noticed something amiss. He found us unmindful. Looking over his shoulder, he saw that the spot where Damini was sitting and sewing the buttons of a shirt was vacant. He realised that we were wondering why Damini had left without caring to listen to his gospel. He lost the track of his thought. After some time, he could not resist himself from getting up and walking up to Damini's room. Standing at her door, he asked, 'Damini, what are you doing here all alone? Won't you like to come to the other room?'

Damini replied, 'No, I have something else to do.'

The Guru peeped in and saw that there was a kite in a cage in the room. A couple of days back, it had got entangled in the telegraph wire and fallen to the ground injured. Damini had rescued it from the pack of crows and had been nursing it for the last two days.

Apart from the kite, Damini had adopted a street puppy also. It was as ugly as low in pedigree. At the slightest sound of the cymbals it raised its head towards the sky and howled in protest. Luckily God did not hear it, but it was a curse for those who did.

One day, when Damini was tending her flowering plants in a broken pot at a corner of the roof, Sachis accosted her and asked, 'Why have you totally stopped going there?'

'Where?'

'In Guruji's quarter.'

'Why do you need me there?'

'We don't need you, but you may need some of those gospels.'

Damini flared up and said, 'No, I don't. None at all.'

Sachis looked at her face, astounded. After a few moments, he gathered himself and said, 'Look, your mind is disturbed. If you want to find peace—'

'How can you give me peace? You people are raising wave upon wave in your mind, day in and day out like madcaps. Where is your peace? I beg of you, leave me alone. I was at peace, I will remain at peace.'

Sachis argued, 'You may be seeing waves on the surface, but if you dive deep with patience, you will find how calm it is.'

Damini folded her palms and said, 'For god's sake, do not ask me to dive any deeper. I will survive if only you people give up on my salvation.'

2

I do not have sufficient experience to pierce the mystery of a woman's heart. Whatever I have realised from the surface, whatever I have seen as an outsider, I have developed this notion that they are ready to lose their heart wherever grief awaits them. They would string their garlands for such a beast, who would crush it under the weight of his base lust. Alternatively, they would adore such a man around whose neck their garland would not reach, for he is steeped in such lofty ideals that his material existence is very thin.

When they choose a life-partner, women leave out men like me who are mediocre by nature, made of both coarse and fine elements, who consider women as women, that is, neither as dolls made of clay nor as pure notes of the veena. They reject us because we cannot offer them either the all-consuming passion of lust or the colourful illusion of dreams. We can neither crush them under the weight of our base desire nor mould them in the cast of our own image by melting them in the heat of our contemplation. We know them for what they are. Hence, even if they like us, they can never love us.

We are their real shelter; it is on our steadfastness that they could depend upon. Our sacrifice is so easy and spontaneous that they tend to ignore its value. Our only reward is that they remember us in their need and perhaps even respect us—but let that pass. Perhaps all this is my anguished thought; or maybe all this is not even true; maybe our victory lies in the fact that we do not get anything in return. At least this train of thought give us a kind of consolation.

Damini avoided Guruji because of her resentment towards him; she avoided Sachis because of a completely opposite feeling towards him. I was the only person at hand on whom neither resentment nor love applied. As a result, when Damini would get an opportunity, she would go on chatting with me about her past, about her present and also about what she saw or experienced in her different forays in the neighbourhood. There was a covered terrace in front of our room where she would sit and crack the betel-nuts with a cutter and keep on babbling to herself under her breath.

I could not even imagine that such a trivial matter would attract the attention of Sachis who was supposed to have been lost in his world of ecstasy. I thought that in Sachis's world all such trifles were illusions of our daily intercourse. People dwelling in that non-illusory world constantly listened to the tune of Lord Krishna's eternal flute floating in from the cosy bank of the Jamuna. The ephemeral episodes of this mundane world did not appeal to their eyes or ears. At least, before our return from the cave, Sachis's level of consciousness was on that higher plane.

Of course, I was also at fault. I had started occasionally playing truant from our sessions on divine love with Guruji. Sachis did not fail to notice that. One day he caught me running after Damini's pet mongoose with a pot of milk bought from the milkman for feeding it. This was a very poor excuse for not attending the session; at least it could have been postponed till the session was over. As a matter of fact, it would have been a better act of kindness to the animal if the responsibility of the mongoose satisfying its hunger were left to itself. Hence, I was embarrassed to suddenly come face to face with Sachis. Putting the pot down where I stood, I tried to salvage my self-respect by sneaking out of the place.

But Damini caught me on the wrong foot. Completely at ease, she asked me loudly, 'Where are you going, Sribilas-babu?'

I scratched my head and mumbled, 'Well, I thought...'

Damini said, 'Their kirtan is over by now. You please sit here.'

This rather intimate entreaty of Damini in presence of Sachis made my ears hot.

Damini now addressed Sachis, 'There is a little problem with the mongoose. It has consumed a hen from the house of our Muslim neighbour last night. So, it cannot be kept at large any more. I have asked Sribilas-babu to buy me a large wicker-basket to keep it in.

It seemed Damini was a little too keen to advertise before Sachis my loyalty to her in the matter of feeding milk to the mongoose or buying a basket for it. I was reminded of the day when Guruji asked Sachis to make his tobacco in front of me. This was the same strategy.

Sachis left the place hurriedly without saying a word. Damini's eyes flashed like lightning looking at his retreating figure. A sardonic smile crossed her lips.

I could not fathom what was playing in Damini's mind. From that day onwards she started sending for me for every little chore. At the same time, she would often herself prepare a sweet dish and sit down to specially feed me. If I said, 'What about Sachis?', she would reply, 'He would feel unnecessarily disturbed if I called him to eat.'

At times, Sachis would pass by and notice me eating in Damini's room.

Between the three of us, my condition was the most precarious. Two major characters of this play were acting from behind the curtain, whereas I was the only public character. The only reason for this was that mine was a minor role. I cursed my fate, and yet I could not resist the temptation of all the affection that was being lavished on me. This was a real dilemma.

3

For a few days on, Sachis went about singing and dancing and playing the cymbals with more gusto. Then one day he came to me and said, 'We cannot keep Damini with us anymore.'

'Why?' I asked.

He replied, 'We have to totally shun the company of Prakriti (woman).'

I said, 'If you think so, I would conclude that there is something terribly wrong in our spiritual discipline.'

Sachis stared at me with full attention.

I continued, 'What you are calling Prakriti is a real entity. Even if you want to exclude her, she will not be excluded from the world we live in. Hence, if you keep doing your 'sadhana' as if she does not exist, then you will be merely deceiving yourself; the day the deceit is exposed, there will be no escape route for you.'

Sachis retorted, 'Enough of this theoretical argument! I am talking about a practical situation. It is obvious that women are agents of Prakriti. It is to obey Nature's bidding that they try to win us over by their artful ways. Unless they overpower our consciousness, they cannot fulfil the design of their mistress. Hence, if we want to keep our consciousness pure, we have to avoid these agents of Nature as far as practicable.'

I was about to say something, but Sachis stopped me and continued, 'My dear Sri, you are unable to see the wiles of Nature because you are already caught in her snare. The beauty with which she has charmed you today is a mask that she would throw away once her purpose is served. The very longing for which you are finding this beauty to be the most important thing in this world will be snuffed out by her the moment your time is up. What then is the point of daring into such a situation where the trap of illusion is laid with such dexterity?'

I replied, 'I agree to all that you say, but my only point is that I have not laid this trap of Nature throughout the world, nor do I know where to go by-passing it. Since we have no way of ignoring its existence, then the best path of sadhana will be to acknowledge it and then try to rise above it. Whatever you say, we are not leading in that path and hence, we smart under the desire to clip half the truth.'

Sachis said, 'Tell me in a little more detail what precisely is your idea of sadhana.'

I replied, 'We have to steer our boat of life up the current of Nature. It should not be our option to evade the current; our aim should be to keep the boat sailing. That is why we need a rudder.'

Sachis countered, 'As you do not put faith in the Guru, you do not know that it is the Guru who is that rudder. If you want to course the path of sadhana according to your whim, you will be lost.'

Having said this, Sachis went into the Guru's room and started massaging his feet. Later, he prepared the tobacco for Guru's hookah and lodged a complaint against the Prakriti.

The deliberations did not end in one day's round of tobacco. The Guru gave the matter a serious thought through the following days. Damini had given him a lot of trouble. Now it seemed this one girl had also created a cyclone among his disciples and their steady stream of spiritual life. But he was at a loss to decide where to relocate Damini, because Sibatosh had pledged Damini also to him along with all his property. More importantly, the Guru was scared of Damini.

Meanwhile, Sachis's fervour for bhakti was redoubled these days; he would regularly massage the Guru's feet, would repeatedly make his tobacco; and yet he could not get rid of the feelng that Prakriti had firmly positioned herself on the path of his sadhana.

One evening, a famous foreign troupe gave a kirtan recital at the temple of Govindaji. We were all there and it was obvious that the *naam-kirtan* would continue till late at night. I sneaked out of the gathering after some time, not imagining that my absence would be noticed by anyone.

That evening Damini laid her heart bare to me. She even expressed in smooth and graceful tongue such topics which we usually did not express even if we wanted to. It seemed that while talking, she herself discovered for the first time many secret and unknown chambers of her mind, as though she found an opportunity to stand face to face with herself.

We did not even know when Sachis had come and stood behind us. Tears were then flowing freely out of Damini's eyes. It was not that she was saying something very significant. But that evening, all her words spurted out of the depth of her tears.

When Sachis came, the kirtan recital could not have been over. I realised that something was constantly driving him from within. Suddenly seeing Sachis there, Damini wiped her tears and made for the adjacent room. With a quivering voice Sachis called her back, 'Listen Damini, I want to tell you something.'

Damini slowly sat down again. As I was about to get up and leave, she threw me such a look that I could not even move.

Sachis said, 'You have not come to Guruji with the same urge with which we have.'

Damini replied, 'No.'

Sachis asked, 'Then why are you staying with all these devotees?'

Damini's eyes flashed with anger; she said, 'Why am I here? Am I here at my own sweet will? You devotees have put a chain round the feet of this woman without faith and put her in your prison of devotion. Have you left any other way open for me?'

Sachis declared, 'We have decided that you may go and live with a relative. We will bear all the expenses.'

'You have decided?'

'Yes.'

'But I have not.'

'Why, what is your inconvenience in this arrangement?'

'One of you will decide something for me, another of you will decide something else—all to suit your convenience. Am I a mere pawn in your chessboard?'

Sachis stared at her in surprise.

Damini continued, 'I have not joined you at my own accord hoping that you people will like me. But I will not move anywhere else just because you people do not like me.'

As she said so, she burst into sobs, stuffing the corner of her sari in her mouth to suppress her sobbing. Almost immediately she rushed to her room and shut the door from inside.

That evening, Sachis did not go back to the session of kirtan. He sat down on the terrace silently. That evening, the distant sound of the waves of the sea was borne by the southern wind towards the stars like the deep wailing from the bosom of the earth. I went out in the dark and roamed the solitary path of the village.

4

The heaven of spiritual joy in which Guruji tried to tie us down was being threatened to be destroyed by the mundane world today. So long, he had made us drink the wine of ecstasy from the allegorical container, but now a clash with the physical was about to topple that container to the ground. He was not unaware of the signs of imminent catastrophe.

Sachis was now a different person. Like a paper-kite whose string had snapped, he was still floating in the wind, but was soon to fall flat on the ground. Although he did not skip any of the regular disciplines like meditation, deliberation, worshipping and singing the name of the Lord, his eyes betrayed a lack of conviction.

As for my position, Damini left no one in doubt about it. The more she realised that the Guruji was scared and Sachis was agitated the more she started demanding my attention openly. Suppose Sachis and I were having some discussion with the Guruji, Damini would come near the door and call out, 'Sribilas-babu, please come for a minute.' She would not bother to say what she wanted of me. Guruji would look at me, Sachis would look at me, I would hesitate for a moment and then would abruptly get up and leave the room. Even after I had left, they would try to continue the discussion for a while, but eventually it would be evident that they had lost the thread. In this way, things started becoming rather disorderly, pieces were not falling into place any more.

Sachis and I were Guruji's chief mounts, almost like Lord Indra's celestial elephant and steed. Hence, he could not give up on us easily. One day he went up to Damini and told her, 'Look, my child, this time I am planning a rather long and difficult trip. You may have to get back from here.'

'Where shall I go?'

'To your aunt's place.'

'That's not possible.'

'Why?'

'First, she is not my real aunt; secondly, why should she accept my responsibility?'

'We'll arrange that she need not bear your expenses—'

'It's not the question of expenses only. She is under no obligation to look after me.'

'How can I look after and keep you with me forever?'

'Am I obliged to answer this question?'

'Where will you go if I die?'

'Nobody has given me the responsibility of thinking about it. What I have been told is that I have no mother, no father, no brother; I have no home, no money, nothing. This is why I am a heavy burden. You have taken that burden at your own will. Now you cannot unburden it on somebody else's shoulder.'

Having said so, Damini left the place. Guruji heaved a long sigh, muttering, 'O Lord.'

One day, Damini ordered me to get for her a few good Bengali books. It goes without saying that by 'good' books, she did not mean any devotional treatise like Narahari Chakrabarti's *Bhakti-Ratnakar* (The Jewel-filled Ocean of Devotional Service). She would never think twice to make such claims on me. In her own way, she guessed that as far as I was concerned, making demands was akin to bestowing favour. Some trees fared better if their branches were pruned. For Damini, I belonged to that category.

The author whose books I got for Damini was an unadulterated modernist. The stamp of Man rather than of Manu was more in his writing. The packet of books fell in Guruji's hands. He frowned and asked, 'Well, Sribilas, why have you got these books?'

I remained silent.

Guruji leafed through a couple of books and said, 'I do not see any hint of sublime thoughts in these.'

I softly said, 'Maybe you will find the hint of sublime thought if you read them carefully.'

As a matter of fact, a revolt was brewing within me. I was totally exhausted by the aftermath of devotional intoxication. I had had enough of this constant dissection of human sensibility by forgetting the real man himself.

Guruji stared at my face for a few moments. Then he said, 'Alright, then it calls for a little more detailed attention.' He kept the books under his pillow. I realised that he had no intention of handing them over.

Damini must have overheard the conversation from the other side of the door. Now she appeared near the door and asked me, 'Haven't you brought the books that I wanted you to get?'

I remained silent.

Guruji said, 'My dear, those books are not worthy of you.'

Damini asked, 'How would you know?'

Guruji frowned and countered, 'How would you for that matter?'

'I have read them earlier. Perhaps you have not.'

'Then why do you need them again?'

'When you need something you get it. It is only in my case that there should not be any need, right?'

'You know that I am a monk, a renunciator.'

'And you know that I am not. I should like to read those books. Please give them to me.'

Guruji pulled out the books from under the pillow and threw them near me. I passed them on to Damini.

As a fall-out of this incident, Damini gave up her earlier practice of reading the books by herself, and started sending for me to read them out to her. We would sit in the open veranda, read and discuss them. Sachis would often cross up and down, perhaps even think of sitting down, but feel shy of joining uninvited.

One day, on hearing a particularly amusing passage in one of the books, Damini broke out in loud laughter. On that day, there was a fair by the temple. We thought that Sachis had gone there. But suddenly the doors from the other side opened. Sachis came out and sat down with us.

Damini's laughter immediately died down. I was also a little flustered. I would have liked to open a conversation with Sachis, but could not find a topic. I kept on silently thumbing the pages of the book. Sachis left as abruptly as he came. Our reading session did not progress any further that day. Perhaps Sachis did not realise that while he envied me for the easy informality of my relationship with Damini, I envied him for the mystery between his and Damini's relationship.

The same day, Sachis went to Guruji and entreated, 'My Lord, I want to spend a few days alone by the seaside; will return in a week's time.'

Guruji responded with enthusiasm, 'Good, you can proceed.'

After Sachis left, Damini stopped calling me for the reading sessions. She did not need me for anything else either. I did not see her going out to interact with the women of the neighbourhood also. She stayed back in her room and the door of the room was always closed.

A few days passed. One afternoon, when Guruji was having a nap and I was writing a letter sitting on the veranda, Sachis suddenly appeared. Without even looking at me, he knocked hard on Damini's doors and called, 'Damini! Damini.'

At once, Damini flung open the door and came out. Sachis was looking miserable, like a ship with broken mast and torn sail, having been caught in a terrible storm; his eyes were dilated, hair unkempt, face pale and clothes soiled.

Sachis said, 'Damini, I told you to go away. It was a mistake. Please forgive me.'

Damini folded her palms and replied, 'Why are you speaking like this?'

'No, you have to forgive me. I will never again repeat the mistake of even thinking that we can keep you or throw you out at our will for the convenience of our sadhana. But I have a request for you and you have to agree to it.'

Damini immediately knelt down and touching his feet she said, 'Your wish is my command.'

Sachis requested, 'Please join us. Do not keep yourself away from our activities.'

Damini obediently said, 'I will be with you. I shall never transgress.' She again bowed down before Sachis's feet and repeated, 'I will not give you any opportunity to complain.'

5

The hard stone melted again. The unbearable fire within Damini now retained only its light, but not the heat. A flower of sweetness blossomed in her service and worship. She was never absent from any kirtan session, nor when Guruji would sit with us for a discourse, nor when he would explain the meaning of the Gita or the *Bhagavat*. Even her dress and demeanour changed. Once again she donned her *tassar* sari. At any time of the day she would look like she had just taken a bath.

Her greatest ordeal was how she conducted herself with the Guruji. When she bowed to him, I would still detect a flash of defiance in the corner of her eyes. I knew for certain that she did not care for any of Guruji's commands, but she surrendered to all his demands with so much submissiveness that one day he even dared to voice his objections about those trash novels by the modern Bengali writer. Next day, he found a bunch of flowers near the bed where he took rest in the afternoon; the flowers were arranged on the torn pages of those books.

I had observed on many occasions that Damini was most irritated when Guruji put Sachis to his own personal services. She often tried to forcibly take over the work of Sachis, but it was not always possible. So, when Sachis blew on the tinder to make Guruji's hookah, Damini would furiously tell herself, 'I would not transgress, I should not transgress.'

But things did not work according to Sachis's liking. Earlier, once when Damini was tamed like this, he saw only her grace, not the real person who embodied it. This time Damini herself had transformed into such a reality that she appeared before his eyes pushing aside all the strains of the kirtan or all the moral precepts of the Guruji. Sachis could see her so vividly that the trance of his divine intoxication was immediately broken. He could no longer conceive her as a metaphor of divine ecstasy. Now, Damini did not enhance the beauty of the songs any more, rather the songs decorated her.

Let me mention a minor fact here. Damini no longer needed me. All her demands on me had suddenly stopped. Among the few companions that I had, the kite had died, the mongoose had escaped and the puppy had been gifted away as it disturbed the Guruji too much. Rendered unemployed and companionless, I again joined the sessions of Guruji, although all its usual discourses and musical performances left me cold.

6

One day, Sachis was busy forming a concoction of all the philosophy, science and theories of the East and the West, of the past and the present in the vast cauldron of his imagination when Damini came running and said, 'Both of you please come with me immediately.'

I sprang to my feet and asked, 'What has happened?'

Damini replied, 'Nabin's wife has consumed poison.'

Nabin was a relative of one of Guruji's disciples. He was not only our neighbour, but a good singer in our kirtan team. On reaching there, we found that his wife had already died. On enquiry, we learnt that Nabin's wife had brought her orphan sister to her house. They were *kulin* (high caste) Brahmins; hence to find a groom for her was difficult. The girl was reasonably good-looking. Nabin's brother had agreed to marry her. He was pursuing his college studies in Calcutta. It was settled that after his exams were over, he would come and marry her in the month of Ashadh (July). Meanwhile, Nabin's wife discovered that her husband and her sister were mutually attracted to each other. So, she insisted that Nabin marry her sister. Much persuasion was not needed and the marriage was solemnised. Once it was over, Nabin's wife committed suicide by taking poison.

There was nothing much to be done. So, we returned. A lot of disciples flocked to Guruji. They started singing kirtan for his benefit. He joined them and started dancing in a daze.

The moon had risen in the sky. Damini was sitting silently in the light and shade created by the *chalta* tree overhanging a corner of the roof. Sachis was slowly pacing up and down the covered corridor behind her. I was writing my diary sitting alone in the room.

That night the cuckoo never slept. It was as if the leaves of the tree were murmuring to each other in the southern breeze, and the moonlight glistened on them. Suddenly Sachis stopped pacing and stood behind Damini. She started, covered her head with the border of her sari and got up to go, when Sachis called, 'Damini!'

Damini stopped short. Then she folded her palms and said, 'My Lord, tell me something.'

Sachis looked at her face intently. Damini continued, 'Please explain to me how the world will be benefited by what you people are doing day and night. Could you save anyone?'

I came out of the room and stood on the veranda. Damini said, 'You are talking about divine love day in and day out. There is nothing else on your lips. Have not you seen today what it exactly is? It does not care for any religion or duty; it does not have brother or wife, society or family; lineage or respect; it knows no kindness, no faith, no shame. What ways have you devised to save mankind from this utterly cruel, brazen and shameless divine love?'

I could not resist myself and blurted out, 'We have devised the policy of practising safe divine love by banishing women from our parameter.'

Without paying any heed to my caustic comment, Damini told Sachis, 'I have not benefitted at all from your Guru. He has not been able to calm my restless mind. You cannot extinguish fire with fire. The path along which your Guru is leading all of you does not have either courage or strength or peace. The girl who died is a victim of this demoness of love. Have not you seen its ugly face? I beg of you with folded palms, please do not put me on the altar of sacrifice to that demoness. Save me. If anyone can deliver me, it is you alone.'

For a few moments all three of us remained silent. Everything around us turned so still that I felt as if the pale sky had turned cold at the sound of the cricket.

At last Sachis asked, 'Tell me what I can do for you.'

Damini replied, 'You be my Guru. I will not listen to anyone else. Give me a *mantra* that is higher than all this nonsense—which can save my soul. Do not let my god perish with me.'

Sachis stood still and said, 'Alright. So be it.'

Damini bowed down at Sachis's feet for a long while, whispering all along, 'You are my Guru, my Guru! Save me from all my trespasses, please save me!'

Epilogue

Another whispering campaign and rounds of slander in the newspapers started that Sachis had again changed his opinion. Once he had loudly denounced religion or caste. Then with equal noise he had started worshipping all the gods and goddesses, performing ablutions and prayers and singing kirtans and bhajans. Now suddenly he again discarded everything and sat down calmly in a meditative mood. It was no longer learnt what he believed in and what he did not. However, everyone could see that he was back at work as before, but totally eshchewing his argumentative self.

The papers also carried a lot of criticism and sarcasm on another issue. Damini and I had got married. But it was not expected that people would know what the mystery was behind this marriage, nor did they need to know.

Sribilas

Once there was an indigo factory here. Now everything is destroyed barring a few rooms of the bungalow. While on my way back after cremating Damini, I took a fancy to this place and decided to stay here for a few days.

The path leading from the river to the bungalow was lined on both sides by rows of *sishu* trees. The garden no longer existed, but the two broken columns of the destroyed gate to the garden stood erect, along with a part of the surrounding wall. There was only the grave of a Muslim factory overseer. In its many crevices there were thick bushes of wild hazel and *akanda* plants. The luxuriant blossoms of their flowers were dancing in the southern breeze like the swaying of the laughing bridesmaids in the bride's chamber. They were as if mocking Death's severity. The banks of the pond had given away. The farmers had utilised this wet spot to cultivate coriander and pigeon-peas. When I sit upon the mossy heap of bricks under the shade of a *sishu* tree in the morning, my senses are numbed by the sweet smell of coriander flowers.

I think of the once vibrant indigo plantation, which today lies like a heap of dry bones in the slaughter-house. No one could have imagined that the waves of joys and sorrows that it generated once upon a time would ever subside. Who am I, a wretched Bengali chap, in front of the mighty Sahib who sat here and turned the blood of thousands of poor peasants into indigo! But Mother Earth, having tucked the green *anchal* of her sari in her waist, had cleaned and shoved everything under the ground today; whatever little relics of the old times are visible now will also be gone when another layer is piled upon them.

But this is an old philosophy. I am not here to repeat it. My mind tells me, no, this is not just the mopping of the courtyard by Time, morning after morning. True, the mighty Sahib and the horror of his indigo cultivation have been wiped away like a speck of dust, but what about my Damini!

I know, nobody will be convinced by what I want to say. The *Moha Mudgara* (Hammer of Delusion) of Shankaracharya does not spare any one. But Shankaracharya was a monk. He talked about the illusion regarding your relationships with your wife and son, but he did not understand the meaning of such relationships. I am not a monk; so I know quite well that Damini was 'no drop of dew on the lotus leaf'.

I hear that some worldly people also talk of such renunciation. Perhaps it is possible. But they are just householders. When they lose their homemaker, their home becomes an illusion, and so is the homemaker. Those are make-believe stuff, one broomstick is good enough to sweep them away.

I did not find time enough to become a householder proper. And mercifully, renunciation is not my cup of tea. So, one whom I got with me did not turn into a 'housewife', but she was not an illusion either. She remained real, she remained Damini till the end. Who dares to call her an illusion?

If I had known Damini only as my wife I would not have written so much about her. But I have known her beyond that social relationship as a true person. This is why I am able to write everything candidly without caring for public opinion.

If I could spend my life with Damini, like people do in this illusory world, I could have remained happy with daily routine of oil-massaging, bathing, eating and sleeping at regular intervals. And after Damini's death, I would have heaved a sigh saying, 'Life is Maya indeed!' and after a while I would have acquiesced to the entreaties of one of the aunts to remarry and test life's strangeness once again. But I had not entered the business of conjugal life as easily as one's feet slip into an old pair of shoes. I gave up expectation of happiness from the beginning. No, that may not be true—I am not such a dunce to give up all expectations of happiness. I definitely hoped for, but did not lay my claim on it.

Why did I not? Because, it is I who persuaded Damini to marry me. Our eyes had not met in a romantic fashion in the evening twilight as they do in conventional marriages. We did what we did deliberately under broad daylight in full knowledge of everything.

When we left Leelananda Swami we realised that we needed a place to stay and food to eat. So long we had lived a carefree life, stayed in an easily available house and eaten the prasad of Guru to our hearts' content. It might have given indigestion but we never experienced the state of hunger. We totally forgot that one had to build or rent a house and protect it, so that one could live in it. In our days of divine bliss, the onus was on the owner of the house to provide us comfortable rooms to stay. We never bothered to think if our host had enough room left for himself.

Then we remembered that Uncle had willed his house to Sachis. If the document was with Sachis, it would have gone astray by the tide of divine ecstasy that we went through so long. But the will was with me; I was its executor. There were a few terms and conditions in the will and it was my responsibility to see that these were fulfilled. Three major ones were the following; there should not be any worship of gods and goddesses in this house; a night school had to be started on the ground floor for the Muslim and *chamar* boys; and after Sachis's death, the entire house should be donated for their education and welfare. Uncle had the greatest apathy towards piety; he considered it murkier than materialism. So he took these measures to counter the thick wind of piousness coming from the other side of the house. He used to call this practice 'sanitary precautions'.

I told Sachis, 'Let us go to our house in Calcutta.'

Sachis replied, 'I am not yet prepared for it.'

I did not fully understand the meaning of his statement.

He continued, 'Once I relied on my intellect. But I realised that it did not account for all aspects of life. Then I depended on faith, but realised that it did not have any basis whatsoever. Intellect is mine, so is the devotion. One cannot lean on one's own structure. Unless I find something better to lean on, I do not dare to return to the city.'

I asked, 'What do you want us to do?'

He advised, 'You two go there. I would wander alone for a few days. I feel as if I have a shore in sight. If I lose the direction now, I will never be able to find it again.'

Damini took me aside and said, 'We can't let this happen. Who will look after him if he wanders alone? I shudder to think of his wretched state last time, when he returned from a solo trip.'

Let me confess. This concern of Damini stung me sharply like an angry bee. Sachis travelled alone for two years after Uncle's death, but did he not survive? Unable to suppress my indignation, I blurted it out, coloured with some strong emotions.

Damini said, 'Sribilas-babu, I grant that people do not die easily. But as long as we are there, why should we allow him to suffer?'

We! At least half of this plural was meant for this wretched Sribilas. Some people in this world have to suffer to save some other people from suffering. The world comprises these two types of people. Damini had easily understood which type I belonged to. But I was happy that she had at least counted me on her side.

I went up to Sachis and told him, 'Well, it's not necessary that we go to the city right away. There is an abandoned house by the side of the river. Let us go and stay there for a few days. It is rumoured that the house is haunted. So, at least we have the guarantee that mankind will not disturb you!'

Sachis asked, 'And what about you?'

I replied, 'We would stay as unobtrusively as possible like the ghosts.'

Sachis looked at Damini for a moment. There was a lurking apprehension in his gaze.

Damini folded her hands and pleaded, 'You are my Guru. I may be a sinner, but please give me the right to serve you.'

2

Whatever you say, I did not quite comprehend this great urge of Sachis for seeking the truth. There was a time when I laughed away this restlessness. Now even my derisive laughter had stopped. This was not the flare of a will-o'-the-wisp, but real fire. When I observed how Sachis was burning, I lost the nerve to proffer Uncle's arguments to him. What is the point of grappling with Herbert Spencer's theories about probability and improbability, when I could clearly see the simmering fire roasting Sachis! His life from start to end was all ablaze.

So long he had been restlessly moving about, singing bhajans, dancing with kirtans to please his Guru. He would suppress all the natural urges of his mind and devote himself totally to the master's will. Now he had decided that the call of the mind should not be ignored. No more submerging oneself in the ocean of ecstasy. His mind was now struggling so hard for realising the self that his face looked dreadfully set.

One day, I could not hold myself any longer and told him, 'Look Sachis, I think you need a Guru under whose guidance your search would be easier.'

Sachis was annoyed and curtly replied, 'Shut up, Sribilas, who wants the easier path? Shortcuts are misleading. Truth is hard to find.'

I tentatively offered, 'You need someone to show the way to Truth.'

Sachis replied exasperatedly, 'My dear, it is not the truth of your geography book. My God walks the path of my soul; the path of a Guru is only meant for walking down to his courtyard.'

How many contradictory things one heard from the mouth of the same Sachis! I, Sribilas, am definitely a disciple of Uncle, but he would have beaten me with a stick had I called him my Guru. The same Sribilas was made to massage Sachis's Guru's feet. Now the same Sachis was lecturing me about the futility of looking for a Guru. I felt like bursting out in laughter, but was scared to do so.

Sachis continued, 'Now I clearly realise the meaning of the *shloka*: *Swadharme nidhanang shreya, paradharma bhoyabhoyah*. It is better to perish by one's own creed than adopt somebody else's. You may borrow everything else from other people, but your dharma should be your own; otherwise it does not protect, but destroys. My God will not come to me as an alm from someone. If I realise him, I will do it on my own. Otherwise, let me perish in the effort.'

I am quite argumentative by nature and do not give up easily. I parried, 'One who is a poet experiences poetry from inside. One who is not a poet has to receive it from someone else.'

Without batting an eyelid, Sachis declared, 'I am a poet.'

There was no scope of any further argument. So, I left the place.

Sachis became extremely erratic. He had no regular time for food or sleep. He roamed about listlessly. He started growing thin and emaciated day by day. I often doubted if he could endure any more. Yet, I did not dare to disturb him. But Damini did. She could not bear to see Sachis's plight. She would get furious with God. She thought He was helpless against those who did not care for Him, but would torture those who were devoted to Him. In the past, whenever she was angry with Leelananda Swami, she used to express it quite strongly, but the problem with God was that He was not easily available for bashing.

Still, she would not give up her attempts to make Sachis bathe and eat in time. She would try out all her tricks to bind this wretched strange man into some regularity.

For a length of time, Sachis did not protest. But one morning, he walked across the river and went to the sand bank on the other side. The sun climbed to the zenith and then tilted to the west, but Sachis was not to be seen. Damini skipped her own meal and waited. At last she lost her patience. Taking the bowl of food in her hand she also crossed the river and walked to the other side.

The place was totally empty and deserted, nothing stirred anywhere. The sun was beating down mercilessly. The sand dunes were also cruel, as if secretly guarding the void.

Damini felt frightened standing in the midst of the endless white sand where no one responded to her calls, no one answered her questions. It was as if a big 'No' was lying under her feet. It had neither sound, nor motion; nor the blue of the sky, nor the green of the vegetation or the ochre of the earth. As if the lipless smile of a skull, as if a huge dry tongue was appealing before the unkind sky to quench its thirst.

As Damini was desperately trying to guess which way to go, she noticed a few footprints on the sand. She followed the footprints and reached a marshland. A number of birds had left their marks on its soft wet shore. Sachis was sitting there on the sand under the shade of a tree. The water in front was deep blue. A few birds were preening their white and golden feathers upon the wet earth. A little further ahead, a noisy flock of birds was constantly trying to smoothen their ruffled feathers. As Damini stepped on the shore they all flew away.

Seeing Damini, Sachis asked peevishly, 'Why have you come here?'

Damini replied, 'I've brought your food.'

Sachis said, 'I don't want to eat.'

Damini argued, 'It is already late.'

Sachis persisted, 'No.'

Damini tried to placate him, saying, 'Alright, I'll wait for a while. Whenever you feel like...'

Sachis rudely said, 'Look, why do you...'

Suddenly looking at Damini's face, he stopped short. Damini did not say anything more. Taking the bowl of food in her hand, she got up and left. The sand all around was burning like the tiger's eyes at night.

Damini's eyes easily lit up with fire, but very seldom did they shed tears. On that evening when I saw her again, she was sitting on the floor with her legs stretched out, water streaming down her eyes. Seeing me, she broke into a fresh flood of tears, breaking through all barriers. My heart ached. I sat down next to her.

After she recovered a little, I asked, 'Why do you worry so much about Sachis's physical well-being?'

Damini replied, 'What else can I worry about? He is thinking of the rest himself. Do I understand any of it?'

I argued, 'Look, when the mind of a man grapples with something very hard, his bodily requirements automatically reduce. This is why, a person loses hunger and thirst when he is too full of joy or sorrow. Seeing the mental turmoil that Sachis is going through, it would not harm if you do not worry too much about his physical needs.'

Damini replied, 'But I am a woman. It is our natural bent to build up this body of flesh and blood with all care. This is an achievement peculiar to womankind. Hence, when we find the body is suffering, our mind cannot bear to see it.'

I said, 'Perhaps this is the reason why those who are preoccupied with their soul do not even glance at you, the caregiver to the body.'

Damini rose to her height and said, 'Of course they do. But they glance at us with such a look which creates havoc.'

I thought, 'And you people are very desirous of such havoc!' I told myself, 'Look, you Sribilas, be pious and righteous in this life so that you can also create such havoc in the next life.'

3

The result of Sachis's rude behaviour with Damini on the bank of the river was that he could not forget her agony-stricken face for a long time. As a mark of repentance, he tried to give special attention to Damini. He had not even properly talked to us for many days, but now he started calling Damini to him and making conversation with her. The subject was always about his innermost thoughts and the probability of his self-realisation.

Damini was not afraid of Sachis's indifference, but she really feared his solicitude. She knew that it was too good to be true for it was too priceless. One day when Sachis would look up the accounts, he would understand that the credit was higher than debit. The danger lay there. These days Sachis took his bath in time and ate his food in time like a good boy. At this, Damini's heart trembled with unknown fear. She also felt a little embarrassed at his change. It was as if she would be relieved if Sachis had played truant. She thought within herself, 'You drove me away the other day. That was better. Your solicitude towards me is like giving punishment to yourself. How can I bear it?'

Damini thought, 'Enough of this! I will have to again make friends with the women of the neighbourhood and start roaming about.'

One night Sachis called us loudly, 'Sri! Damini!' He was totally oblivious of the time, whether it was one or two in the morning. In fact, I could not quite guess what he did through the night. But I was sure the ghosts of this haunted house must have been totally confused by his nocturnal habits.

Jolted out of our sleep, we ran to the veranda and found Sachis standing in the dark cemented terrace of the house. He spoke out, 'I have understood it well. There is not even an iota of doubt in my mind.'

Damini slowly sat down on the terrace. Sachis also absent-mindedly imitated her. So did I.

Sachis said, 'If I walk in the same direction in which He is coming towards me, then gradually my distance with Him will keep increasing. Our union is possible only if I move in the opposite direction.'

I looked at his burning eyes silently. What he said was geometrically correct, but what did he exactly mean?

Sachis continued, 'He loves form, so He is constantly coming down towards form. We do not live with only form, so we have to rush towards the formless. He is free, and therefore revels in bondage; we are bound, so our pleasure is in the freedom. All our sufferings emanate from the fact that we do not understand this simple truth.'

We remained still like the stars in the sky. Sachis explained, 'Damini, don't you understand? The one who sings moves from joy towards rhythm; the one who listens to the song moves from rhythm towards joy. One comes from liberty to binding, the other moves from binding towards liberty. This is how the two sides unite. He is singing and we are listening.'

I did not know if Damini understood what Sachis said, but she understood Sachis. She sat silently with her palms folded in her lap.

Sachis said, 'So long I have been listening to the song of that Master. Suddenly I realised everything. I could not resist the temptation of waking you up and sharing it. All these days were wasted in moulding Him in my own shape. O my destroyer, I will keep shattering my self in million fragments and merge in you for ever. I cannot stick to any bond, because binding is not for me; but binding is for you, so you could never extricate yourself out of the bond of your own Creation. Be there with my form. I will dive into your formlessness.'

Sachis rose and walked away in the dark to the riverside, chanting, 'O Infinity! You are mine, you are mine.'

4

From that night onwards, Sachis went back to his earlier waywardness. There was no regularity in his daily life. I could not even gauge when his mind rushed towards light and when it plunged into darkness. God help the person who had taken the responsibility of keeping such a whimsical man within the domesticity of regular bath and meal.

After a sultry day, suddenly there broke a terrible storm at night. Three of us used to sleep in three adjacent rooms, with a kerosene lamp burning in the veranda in front. The lamp was blown out. The river rose in spate, the sky broke out in torrents of rain. The lapping sound of the waves of the river combined with the sound of the falling raindrops and rang loud like cymbals in the deluge. One could not see what moved in the womb of the thick darkness, yet its various sounds made the sky shiver in the bone and tremble like a blind and frightened lad. The bamboo clumps moaned like a lonely spirit. The sound of the fallen leaves and branches in the mango grove, the sound from afar when a part of the banks of the river gave away and the sound of the whistling wind cutting through crevices of our dilapidated house—all combined to raise a great din, almost like an animal's howl.

On such nights, the bolts and locks of the doors and windows of our minds are torn away. The storm raids the interiors, throws all the genteel furniture into a disarray, blows the curtains in all directions and sweeps through everything. I could not sleep. What I was thinking while tossing in the bed is of no consequence here.

Suddenly Sachis called out from the darkness of his room. 'Who is there?'

The reply came, 'It's I, Damini. The windows in your room are open, the rain is blowing in. I am closing them.'

While doing so, Damini saw that Sachis was sitting on the bed. He hesitated for a moment and then bolted out of the house in the stormy night. The lightning flashed, the thunder roared.

Damini sat on the threshold of her room for a long time. No one returned. The impatience of the bursts of wind only kept increasing.

Damini could not stand it any more. She went out. It was difficult to stand steady in the gust of wind. It seemed the messengers of the wind-god were reproachfully pushing her forward. Today the darkness was almost mobile. The rain-water was as if trying to fill up all the corners of the universe. Perhaps Damini would have been relieved if she could cry like this.

Suddenly a flash of lightning ripped through the sky with a thundering sound. In that momentary light Damini saw Sachis standing near the river, Damini marshalled all her energies to run the distance and fell at his feet. Defeating the sound of the wind she cried, 'Here I touch your feet and say that I have not transgressed as far as you are concerned. Then why are you punishing me like this?'

Sachis stood still. Damini said, 'If you wish, you can kick me down into the river, but please get back to the house.'

Sachis returned to the house. The first thing he uttered on return was, 'I desperately need the One whom I am searching for. I don't need anything else. Damini, have pity on me, and leave me for ever.'

Damini remained silent for a while. Then she said, 'Yes, I will leave.'

5

I heard all these details from Damini later, but did not know any of this on that day. Hence, as I watched both walking through the veranda towards their respective bedrooms, I felt as if my ill fate had climbed upon my chest and was trying to stifle me. I sat up on the bed with a jolt and could not go back to sleep.

Next morning, Damini looked devastated. It looked as if the *tandava* dance of last night's storm had left all its footprints on her. Even without knowing what had exactly transpired, I was angry with Sachis.

Damini requested me, 'Sribilas-babu, will you please escort me to Calcutta?'

I knew how difficult it was for Damini to make this request, yet I did not ask her anything. Even in the midst of great pain, I felt some relief. It was better for Damini to leave this place. Her boat was already ravaged by constant collisions with the rock.

At the time of taking leave, Damini bowed down at Sachis's feet and said, 'I've committed many sins, please forgive me.'

Sachis kept his eyes down on the ground and replied, 'I've also badly transgressed. Will beg forgiveness from you after washing my sins off.'

On my way to Calcutta, I could very well realise that a raging fire was consuming Damini. One day, the flame of that fire heated my mind also to such an extent that I uttered some harsh words directed towards Sachis. Damini immediately flared up, 'Look, do not say such things about him in my presence. What do you know about the way he saved my soul? You only perceive my sorrow; you do not see the great sorrow that he suffered in his attempt to save me. The ugly had been kicked on the chest because it tried to kill the beautiful. Serves her right, serves her right'—so saying Damini started beating her own chest. I had to press her hands to stop her.

On reaching Calcutta at dusk, I dropped Damini at the house of one of her aunts and checked in at an old mess previously known to me. When I met with an acquaintance, he was stunned to look at my face and said, 'My God! What's happened to you? Are you ill?'

Next day, I received a letter from Damini, 'Please take me away. I am unwanted here.'

The aunt would have nothing to do with Damini. It seemed the whole city was agog with our adultery. A little after we had broken away from our group, the weekly papers came out with special Puja numbers. We had been thoroughly exposed there as immoral and wayward. In Hindu shastra, the sacrifice of a female animal is prohibited, but in case of humans, this was practised with a lot of glee. Though Damini's name was not directly mentioned, there were enough tell-tale hints to identify her as the culprit. So, the aunt's house turned into a curfew zone for her.

Meanwhile, Damini's parents had passed away. I was aware of a couple of her brothers, but Damini was not willing to go to them. When I asked her, she said, 'They are very poor.'

In fact, Damini did not want to put them in trouble. They also must have heard about her waywardness. If they also turned her away, she would not be able to bear the hurt.

I asked, 'Then where will you go?'

She replied, 'To Leelananda Swami.'

I was too stunned to speak for a few moments. What a strange game Destiny was playing!

I expressed my doubt, 'Will he take you back?'

Damini confidently replied, 'Gladly.'

Damini was a keen reader of human character. Those who belong to the business of religion, they would be happier to find a follower rather than finding the truth. It was indeed true that Damini would have no problem in staying at Leelananda Swami's place. But—

At this moment of crisis, I said, 'Damini, there is a way out. If you promise that you won't be angry, I can share it with you.'

Damini said, 'Tell me.'

I said, 'If it's possible for you to marry a person like me...'

Damini stopped me, saying, 'What are you saying, Sribilas-babu? Have you gone mad?'

I said, 'Well, why don't you assume that I've gone mad? Once mad, one attains the ability to easily solve many tough problems. Madness is like that pair of slippers of the *Arabian Nights*, wearing which one can easily skip over thousands of worthless things of this world.'

'Worthless things? Like?'

'Like, what will people say, what will happen in the future, etc.'

Damini asked, 'And what about the real issues?'

I counter-questioned, 'What do you mean by real things?'

'Like what misery will befall you, if you marry me?'

'If this is the real question, then I am quite relieved. For, my condition cannot be worse than what it is now.'

I refused to believe that Damini was not at all aware of my feelings towards her. But so long, this was not an important issue to her; at least she was not obliged to respond. Now, after so many days, a demand for response arose.

Damini was thinking silently. I continued, 'Damini, I am a very ordinary man in this world—even less than that, a wretched being. Marrying me will not make any difference in your life. So, you need not worry.'

Damini's eyes were full of tears. She said, 'I would not have worried at all, had you been an ordinary person.'

After a little more of thoughtful silence, Damini added, 'You know me well, don't you?'

I replied, 'You also know me well.'

This is how the marriage proposal was broken. Much more remained unsaid than was said.

Once I had charmed a lot of people by my speeches delivered in English. Due to a long gap, many of those followers had been cured of their devotion to me. But Naren still considered me a genius born with God's grace. One of his houses was vacant for a month and a half. For the time being, we got shelter in that house.

My proposal seemed to have fallen in a ditch of silence like the broken wheel of a carriage. I thought it had got stuck in between 'yes' and 'no' and would take a lot of effort to drag it out of the ditch of silence. But with a supreme sense of irony God created the human mind to beat the psychologists. And now, the roaring laughter of the Creator reverberated on the walls of the rented house in that month of Falgun.

Damini had so long not found time to notice me as a separate man; perhaps the light that fell on her eyes from another source was too bright. Now, her whole world shrank to a space where I was alone. So she had no other alternative but to focus her eyes full on me. I was fortunate that this was exactly when Damini seemed to see me for the first time.

I had walked side by side with Damini over many hills, by many rivers, on many sea-beaches. There were ecstatic kirtans sung loudly on that journey, accompanied by the beat of drums and cymbals. The air was ablaze with songs like, 'The loop of love tightens around my heart, with your feet as my final destiny.' The sparks flew, but the curtain dividing us never caught fire.

But, lo and behold, what had happened in this narrow lane of Calcutta! Those back-to-back houses closing in around us seemed to have blossomed like *parijat* flowers. God definitely demonstrated a miracle by turning the brick and wood into the melody of music. And with what philosopher's stone He touched me, so that I magically turned into an extraordinary person overnight!

When there is a partition, the distance seems eternal, but when the partition is torn down, it is only a moment away. Damini confessed, 'I was passing through a dream, this push was only awaited. In between the you-of-my-past and the you-of-my-present, there was a trance. I bow before my Guru that he has brought me out of this daze.'

I told Damini, 'Please do not gaze at my face so intently. When you earlier discovered that this creation of God is not handsome, I bore it with fortitude. Now, if you discover it again, I won't be able to bear it.'

Damini said, 'I am now discovering the fact that this creation of God is extremely handsome.'

I replied, 'History will remember your name. Your achievement is even grater than the explorer who will plant his flag first at the North Pole. It is not just achieving the difficult, it is achieving the impossible.'

I was never so acutely aware that the month of Falgun was so short. Only thirty days, that too never more than twenty-four hours a day! God has eternity, yet why he was so miserly with time—that beat me!

Damini asked, 'What about your folks? Do they know this mad deed you are going to perform?'

I replied, 'They are my well wishers. They will promptly drive me out of home.'

'And then?'

'Then you and I will construct a new home from the basics. That will be our own creation.'

Damini responded, 'And the mistress of that house also needs to be shaped anew. Let that also be your creation, let nothing of her old self remain as leftover.'

The day of marriage was fixed in the month of Chaitra. Damini insisted that Sachis be fetched for the marriage.

I asked, 'What for?'

'He will ritually give away the bride.'

I had no clue where that crazy fellow was roaming about. Letter after letter sent by me remained unanswered. I was sure he was still staying in that haunted house, otherwise my letters would have been returned. Perhaps he did not even care to open any letter.

I told Damini, 'Look, you may have to personally go and invite him. Letters won't do. I could go alone, but I am the weakling type. Maybe he has gone to the other side of the river to supervise the herons preening their feathers. No one except you can dare to go there.'

Damini laughed and said, 'But I had sworn never to go there again.'

I parried, 'The promise was not to carry food there; but there is nothing wrong in venturing again to invite him to a feast.'

This time there were no dramatic incidents. We took hold of Sachis and brought him to Calcutta peacefully. Sachis was very excited about our wedding, expressing almost a child's joy at receiving new toys. I thought of making it a quiet affair, but Sachis would not hear of it. When he informed all the Muslim followers of the Uncle, they assembled at our place with so much jubilance that people thought the Amir of Kabul or at least the Nizam of Hyderabad had arrived as our wedding guest.

More racket followed in the newspaper. In their next Puja specials there was a double human sacrifice. But we did not curse them. Let the Mother Goddess grace their cash register and let the readers' thirst for human blood be quenched at least for this one occasion.

After everything was over, Sachis decreed, 'Sri, you two go and settle down in my house.'

I entreated, 'You also join us. Let us take a plunge into our social work like earlier days.'

Sachis said, 'No, my work lies elsewhere.'

Although Sachis asked us to go and stay at his house, it turned out to be a tough job. Harimohan had taken possession of the house and rented it out. Perhaps he had desired to occupy it himself, but his spiritual guides warned him against it, since a Muslim had died of plague there. But what about the tenant? Well, this particular information could be suppressed from them.

How the house was rescued from Harimohan's grip is a long story. My chief supporters were the Muslims of the neighbourhood. I just showed them the will of Uncle. After that, I was not required to visit any lawyer's house.

Till then, I always received some financial allowance from my family. This was now discontinued. We two started setting up a proper home without any help. Our pleasure lay in the effort. As a Premchand-Roychand scholar, it was not difficult for me to get a professorship. Over and above, I started churning out thick, made-easy 'guide' books as patent medicines for exams. Our needs were little, it was not necessary for me to toil so hard. But Damini wanted me to make sure that Sachis did not have to worry about earning his livelihood.

There was another issue. Damini's brothers did not have the means to marry off their two daughters to eligible grooms and to prosecute the studies of their sons. I had to take this responsibility without telling Damini anything. Damini also pretended not to know. As regards the brothers, they would not maintain any relationship with us, but that did not prevent them from taking money from me. This was the way of the world!

Hence, I had to find a part-time job of a sub-editor in an English journal. Without consulting Damini, I engaged a cook and a servant. Damini also, without consulting me, dismissed both of them next day. As I protested, she said, 'You people try to be kind without thinking of its effect. You are working tirelessly; if I also do not get to work, where will I hide my grief and shame?'

It was the confluence of the Ganga and the Jamuna—my work outside and Damini's work at home. Over and above, Damini started teaching sewing and seaming to the young Muslim girls of the neighbourhood. As if, she had taken a vow not to be outdone by me.

I do not have the poetic imagination to narrate befittingly how the city of Calcutta became our Vrindavan and how our back-breaking toil became the tune of Krishna's flute. Our days danced away in joy.

One more Falgun passed. But not another.

Damini did not confide in anyone that she had suffered a pain in her chest after our return from that cave. When it aggravated, she responded to my anxious enquiry, saying, 'This pain is my hidden wealth, my touchstone. I could come to you with this dowry, otherwise am I worthy of you?'

The doctors started giving different names to this ailment. Their prescriptions also varied from each other. At last, exhausting all my resources on consultation fees and medicines, they advised me to take her to a healthy place for a change of air. It was like Rama sending Sita into exile after burning down Lanka to reclaim her.

Damini insisted, 'Take me to that seaside, where I have carried the pain from. There is no dearth of fresh air there.'

The night the full moon of Magh passed over to Falgun, the sea swelled up in waves of tears. Damini bowed at my feet and said, 'My desire for you remains unfulfilled in this life. I pray to God that I have you again to myself in the next life.'

Glossary

Akanda: (*Calotropis gigantean*, crown flower, giant milkweed, bowstring hemp, sodom apple, *aak*, *madar*). It is a species native to the Indian subcontinent, South East Asia and tropical Africa. It is a large shrub with clusters of waxy flowers, either white or lavender in colour. The leaves are oval and light green; the stem is milky. Each flower consists of five pointed petals and a small 'crown'. According to the *Shivpuran* the flower is liked by Lord Shiva and offered to him for peace, prosperity and stability. *Calotropis* yields a durable fibre useful for ropes. It helps cure infections, blisters, insect bites and skin diseases. The thick milky juice inside the leaves and stem is also used as an arrow poison and cattle poison. The Shastras also explain that planting the sacred *akanda* plant at the main entrance is highly auspicious.

Anchal: A length of cloth at the end of a draped sari that is left hanging loose over the shoulder and often used to cover the head or draped across the back. Commonly known as *pallu* in the rest of India, the term *anchal* is popular in eastern India.

Babu: A respectful title or form of address for a man, especially an educated one. Used as a suffix to names.

Bhadralok: Traditionally, the worthy, educated and respectable middle class of Bengali people regarded as the custodian of a special value system.

Chalta tree: A large, evergreen tropical tree. Commonly known as the 'elephant apple' or 'chalta' (*Dillenia indica*) this tree is a species native to south eastern Asia. Elephants, deer and monkeys are fond of the fruits, hence the name elephant apple.

Chamar: A *dalit* community now classified as a Scheduled Caste, they were traditionally considered outside the Hindu ranking system of castes known as *varna*. The *chamar* community is often associated with the traditional occupation of tanning and making leather goods.

Kirtan: A devotional song (of Hinduism) typically about the life of Krishna, in which a group repeats lines sung by a leader.

Gol Dighi: This fairly large tank square Gol Dighi in the older and northern part of Kolkata (then Calcutta) came to be known as College Square after David Hare established the Hindu college next to it in 1817.

Mess (Messbari): *Messbari* is an urban Bengali coinage. It is born of the mess, the name for the area where military personnel socialise, eat and live together (*bari* in Bengali means 'home'). The *messbari* or mess culture is an early 19th century phenomenon. These are men's hostels, providing boarding and lodging at fairly cheap rates. These migrant men would rent a room in a *messbari* or a slice of it, depending on availability and affordability.

Moha Mudgara: A popular 8th century Hindu devotional composition in Sanskrit, *Moha Mudgara* (Hammer of Delusion) or *Bhaja Govindam* (Praise/Seek Govinda [Vishnu]) is attributed to Adi Shankara, the Indian theologian who consolidated the doctrine of *Advaita Vedanta*. This work underscores the view that devotion or Bhakti to God (Govinda) is a vastly important part of general spirituality as emphasised by Bhakti Yoga. It is considered a summary of the Advaita Vedanta philosophy.

Naam-kirtan: Similar to kirtan, this involves chanting of the various names of Lord Krishna.

Panda: The people who perform the ritual services at temples in Odisha, especially at the Jagannath temple in Puri are called the *sevayats* (servitors) and the *panda*s work along with them. These Brahmin priests acquire their position hereditarily. Records of 13th century AD and of the British period suggest that there were 36 categories of *sevayats* or *pandas*, which has increased to 250 in the last two centuries.

Parijat: Considered to be a divine tree, the *parijat* (*shefali/shiuli* in Bengali and *harshringar* in Hindi) bears the botanical name *Nycatanthes Arbortristis* and is native to South Asia and Southeast Asia. It is a shrub with a flaky grey bark. This 'night flowering' tree has tales of its romantic origin. A certain princess Parijataka was in love with the sun and when spurned, she committed suicide. A flowering tree sprung from her ashes.

The tree flowers only at night and sheds the pretty white flowers with a bright orange centre, at dawn, forming a carpet of snow-white petals at the feet of the tree.

Prakriti: The prime material energy of which all matter is composed (according to the Vedanta). Symbolises the woman, her beauty and her procreative energy.

Prasad: A devotional offering made to a god, typically consisting of food that is later shared among devotees.

Premchand-Roychand scholarship: This studentship was instituted at the University of Calcutta in 1866 by Premchand-Roychand, a Parsee millionnaire of Bombay (now Mumbai). In terms of emulation and prestige, this scholarship has been the most cherished award for the meritorious students of the Calcutta University pursuing higher studies.

Rain tree flower: *Samanea saman,* also sometimes known as *Albizia saman,* or the rain tree, is a species of flowering tree in the pea family, *Fabaceae,* native to Central and South America. Its range extends from Mexico, south to Peru and Brazil, but it has been widely introduced to South and Southeast Asia. The name 'rain tree' was coined in tropical India, especially Bengal. Its origin is related to the moisture that collects on the ground under the tree, largely the honey-dew like discharge of cicadus feeding on the leaves.

Sadhana: Disciplined and dedicated practice or learning, especially in religion or music. Origin from Sanskrit sadhana, dedication to an aim, from '*sadh*' (wish or passion).

Sishu tree: *Dalbergia sissoo,* commonly known as the North Indian rosewood, is a fast growing and hardy deciduous tree, native to the Indian subcontinent as well as southern Iran. It is a large crooked tree with large leathery leaves and pink flowers.

Sravan: The rainy month during monsoon receiving heavy to very heavy rainfall all across West Bengal, stretching from mid-July to mid-August.

Other translated books of Rabindranath Tagore

Two Sisters
Translated by
Nirmal Kanti Bhattacharjee

Gleanings of the Road
Translated by
Somdatta Mandal

Songs of Tagore
Translated by
Aruna Chakravarti